Masti

One can't get better. – *The Business Standard*

An immensely enjoyable, readable, and gentle book. Kalha Classics are designed to endure ... – *Biblio*

Simple stories of ordinary men and women pulsate with life at Masti's masterly hand. – *The Indian Express*

For those of us who are familiar with the series Katha Prize Stories, this wonderful collection of short stories by Jnanpith award-winning writer, Masti comes as no surprise. This collection measures up to the high standards of excellence set by the earlier titles. – *Indian Review of Books*

... the care that Katha has taken over the format deserves praise.
– *The Economic Times*

SELECT KATHA TITLES

SHORT STORIES

Masti
VENKATESHA IYENGAR

Translated and Edited by
Ramachandra Sharma

KATHA

Katha Classics

KATHA

First published by Katha in 1995

KATHA
A3, Sarvodaya Enclave
Sri Aurobindo Marg, New Delhi 110 017

Phone: (91-11) 4141 6600, 4141 6610

Fax: (91-11) 2651 4373

E-mail: marketing@katha.org

Website: http://www.katha.org

KATHA is a registered nonprofit organization
devoted to enhancing the joy of reading.
KATHA VILASAM is its story research and resource centre.

General Series Editor: Geeta Dharmarajan
In-house Editor: Keerti Ramachandra
Design: Taposhi Ghoshal
Illustrations: Shuddho Basu

Cover Design: Geeta Dharmarajan
Cover Painting: T Vaikuntam

Typeset in 10 on 13pt Baskerville by Suresh Sharma at Katha

Katha regularly plants trees to replace the wood used in the making of its books.

ISBN 978-81-87649-50-2

First Reprint 2012, Second Reprint 2016

Masti Venkatesha Iyengar
June 6, 1891 – June 6, 1986

Masti's home for sixty years

Masti with his family

Sharubg a light-hearted moment with the listeners

Masti enjoys a game of cards

CONTENTS

PREFACE

"Do you know he's the father of the modem Kannada short story?" asks U R Anantha Murthy. He has just got the Masti Award. He is beaming at you, delighted, as if this is a great honour – even bigger than the Jnanpith Award he is to get later.

Who is Masti? Why should an award named after him give so much pleasure to one of the best living writers today?

You go to Masti. And sink with pleasure into simple stories, simply told. Their old world charm, their gentleness hold you and, if you are a writer of sorts, you wonder, How does this writer resist the temptation to portray the angst of existence? Why is reading Masti like holding a paper screw of peanuts, sitting on the Marina Beach and staring out into peaceful waters? Even when Masti disturbs, it is a once-removed disturbance, as if reminding us that every house has a doorstep, every home its unhappiness. So then you ask yourself, Why do the stories linger long after you have read them? Maybe if you can answer all those questions, you have already discovered the reason for the pride in Anantha Murthy's eyes, and the pleasure of reading Masti ... even in translation.

Masti is one of the biggest stars on the Kannada firmament. But, a collection of Masti's stories was last published by the Madras University in 1948, in a translation done by Masti himself. It is Katha's fortune to bring out the next translation of his work, as the first of the Katha Classics.

The genesis of this project, for me, goes back many years to reading my first Marquez and wondering why we did not have good translations of our great storytellers. This was one of the main reasons why I started Katha, a nonprofit publishing house that strives to straddle the worlds of literacy and literature. I had contemplated one volume of translations a year: the *Katha Prize Stories*. But I suppose; being Indian, the lure of the short story is in my blood and Katha has felt impelled and compelled to explore the genre as well as is possible for an organisation that works on an embarrassingly slim budget. Two years ago, the Katha Regional Fiction series was launched with The Southern Harvest (edited by Githa Hariharan). And now the Classics. To showcase the writings of path-breakers and trend-setters, master craftspeople who have made landmark contributions to the growth of Indian literature. We have a galaxy of writers who will appear in translation in the Classics series. In 1996, we publish U R Anantha Murthy, Basheer, Mowni, Suresh Joshi and Vyankatesh Madgulkar.

Our books happen mainly due to the ungrudging help and efforts of the Friends of Katha, a network of about 3000 people who passionately love Indian fiction. They come from different walks of life and it is they who have made it possible and necessary for us to remain quality-conscious. We know their concerns will continue to translate into books that place our good writers where they belong – with storytellers like Jorge Luis Borges and Katherine Mansfield, Isaac Bashevis Singer and Yasunari Kawabata, Nadine Gordimer and Gabriel Garcia Marquez, to name a few.

On behalf of Katha I thank the Masti Trust and especially Shri K Lakshman for giving us permission to translate and publish Masti. The Karnataka Government for giving us a grant that helped start this book off. And Dr Ramachandra Sharma, for continued friendship. To conclude, maybe it does not make commercial sense to publish stories which do not have a modem sensibility. But maybe again, it does, for when you read Masti you realise that his stories and characters are a part of yourself and in them you see a world you want to touch and long to hold. In these days of transient joys, that is a nice feeling to have.

November 1995 Geeta Dharmarajan

INTRODUCTION

I have reason to remember the evening of June 5, 1986. A friend of mine had suggested that we go and see the dramatized version of Masti's novel, *Chikaveera Rajendra*, that evening.

The sky had been heavy with dark clouds all day and a threat of rain. We knew from experience that any June rain that started in the evening was not likely to stop before the next morning. Yet we set out on foot.

On the way, my friend mentioned that Masti's health had taken a turn for the worse, adding that for any man over sixty, the days on either side of his birthday were critical.

We watched the play till Dikshita, the Jois, informs the queen that Chikaveera Rajendra, the king, had Kamsayoga and that he should stay away from his sister's son for at least a year. The rumbling of the clouds in the sky could be heard clearly, offering a fitting backdrop to the tragedy that would unfold on the stage.

We left a little later. Soon after we reached home, it started raining and had not stopped at midnight when I went to bed. It was, I remember, a gentle rain and must have continued till the small hours of the morning. The soundless rainfall would have absorbed the silence that followed Masti's last breath into itself, even as the elements drew the man into themselves.

Masti Venkatesha Iyengar died on June 6, 1986, his ninety-fifth birthday. Two other great men had left this world on their birthdays – the Buddha and Shakespeare.

Masti was born on June 6,1891 into a priestly Brahmin family which had fallen on bad days. His father, the shanbogh of the place by, hereditary right, had lost his position when questions were raised about his management of accounts, and he was forced to make his living as a temporary teacher. Theirs was a hand to mouth existence when Masti started his schooling. He was looked after by his maternal grandfather and uncle, while he continued his studies in Shivarapattana, Malavalli, Mysore and Madras. His childhood and adolescence were marked by acute poverty and by death, a not infrequent visitor to the family. Of the four sons born to his parents, one of them died soon after birth and the other, who was close to Masti during his childhood, died of plague when Masti was still in college at Mysore. His parents and his grandparents had arrived there unexpectedly with the news. Masti's father and grandmother died of the dreaded disease two days later and the boy had to support his widowed mother on the stipend he received as a merit student.

In his autobiography, *Bhava*, Masti recounts his childhood and speaks of the affection and respect which existed among the people of the place. His unswerving faith in God as the spirit that moves everything in the universe must have taken shape when he was still a child. One of his earliest memories, he says, is that of his father, sitting on the pyol, reading shlokas from *Ramayana* to him, as he lay on a mat listening.

Masti was a brilliant student throughout, and he was motivated to do well so that he would not need to depend on the charity of the Brahmin community. After his graduation, he went to Madras to do his MA. There, he decided to take the Mysore Civil Service Examination. As expected, he topped the list, and was appointed an Assistant Commissioner in the service of the Maharaja, on a salary of Rs 200 per month. The boy had come a long way since the days when his father managed the family on a teacher's salary of Rs 5 per month.

Masti was married when he was in college. At twenty-six he started his career as a civil servant in the state of Mysore, and rose steadily during the twenty-six years of his service. At one point he was tipped to become a minister. But when one of his juniors was appointed to a post that was rightfully his, Masti resigned in protest, and devoted the rest of his life to the pursuit of literature.

While in service, Masti travelled all over the state and came into close contact with its people. Early in his career, he had established a reputation for uprightness and fearlessness. His genuine concern for the illiterate poor must have drawn people to him. They must have trusted him with the tales of their lives – of their joys and sorrows, of birth and death, of love and hatred.

Masti and his wife had six daughters. When Masti was thirty-three, he and his wife decided not to share the same bed. Thirty years later, Masti wrote with pride about their resolve and their strength in keeping it Not surprisingly, Masti thanks God for guiding them through those years ...

As in the past, Masti saw death snatch away many of his near and dear ones after he had retired from service. He lost two of his daughters and a son-in-law. His wife died in 1969. His friends still speak of the fortitude he displayed on that occasion, in spite of the grief he must have felt at the passing away of a companion of over six decades. But his unshakeable faith in God as the ultimate power that guides everyone's destiny must have given him the strength to accept these vicissitudes. How else can one explain the ever-present smile on his wrinkled face, and the cheer he spread to everyone around him?

Masti admits to having written a few pieces in English before he switched over to Kannada. It is interesting to speculate on the reasons for this. One of them must have been an incident that took place early in his career as a civil servant. Masti pointed out to a farmer in Mallasandra that he should not have broken a law which had been laid down very clearly. The farmer pleaded ignorance of the law because it was in English. This had a powerful impact on Masti's thinking and probably influenced his decision to work for the promotion of Kannada. It became his life's mission to serve it.

There must have been other influences too. In 1911, his teacher, BM Srikantia, gave a clarion call for the resurgence of Kannada. Speaking of the impact of Sanskrit on the language and of its influence on the sensibility of the Kannada people, he suggested that Kannada literature should look up to English for its possible renewal and move away from its dependence on Sanskrit for inspiration. *Rangana Maduve* ("Ranga's Marriage") which Masti had written in Kannada in 1910, was inspired by the stories in Strand magazine which he came across when he was twenty. They opened his eyes to the possibility of making good literature out of the quotidian events of an ordinary man's life.

Soon after he retired in 1944, Masti launched the monthly magazine, *Jeevana*, and edited it for the next two decades. It was a matter of prestige for a writer to have his piece included in *Jeevana*. A number of leading writers of today had their first efforts see the light of day in that magazine and they have spoken fondly of the encouragement they received from Masti. Through his editorials in *Jeevana*, and his association with the Kannada Sahitya Parish ad, he championed the cause of an integrated land for the Kannada people.

Although Masti was one of the writers who met in Delhi, in the early 1950s to set up the Sahitya Akademi, his relationship with the Akademi was not an untroubled one. When the Akademi decided not to give an award to any book in Kannada one year, since none deserved it, Masti withdrew his translation of Shakespeare's *Hamlet*, scheduled to be published by the Akademi, in protest. He fell out with the Akademi again, when it backed out of its decision to have Masti's novel, *Chennabasavanayaka* translated into other Indian languages. The Akademi's decision was influenced by the objection of some members of the Veerashaiva community, who claimed that the portrayal of the leading characters in it was a slur on their community and their faith. Masti was justifiably furious, and kept away from the body for many years. However, both sides moved gradually towards a reconciliation and Masti accepted the Fellowship of the Akademi in 1974.

Among the important responsibilities Masti took up after he retired from service were the presidents hip of PEN and the editorship of three volumes on Rabindranath Tagore, published in connection with Tagore's centenary celebrations.

When Masti presided over the annual Kannada meet in 1929, he was the youngest writer to be so honoured. In 1956, the Kamataka University conferred an honorary D Litt on him, and the University of Mysore bestowed a similar honour on him in 1977. Among the many awards he received were the Sahitya Akademi award for his *Sanna Kathegalu* – 12, 13 in 1969, the Karnataka Sahitya Akademi Award in 1972 and the Jnanpith Prashasti, the highest literary award in 1983, for his historical novel, *Chikaveera Rajendra*, and for his contribution to Indian literature.

The controversy that surrounded this novel and the award needs to be recorded as it highlights an essential aspect of Masti's character. Once again, a small section of the Veerashaiva community felt that Masti had denigrated their faith by his portrayal of the Veerashaiva king, Chikaveera. The Jnanpith Award Committee seemed inclined to withdraw its reference to the novel and merely mention Masti's contribution to Indian literature. Masti was very upset. He wanted to reject the award. Finally, it was agreed that the reference to the novel would remain.

I remember interviewing Masti for the External Services of All India Radio soon after he received the Award. He was pleased, like any ordinary human being, but obviously he was hurt by the controversy surrounding the book. Masti was the first Kannada writer to translate Basavanna's *Vachanas* into English. We should not have hurt a man like him by accusing him of harbouring casteist prejudices in his heart. Certainly not when he was ninety-two.

Another aspect of the contribution Masti made to Kannada literature, was to promote the publication of good books in Kannada. Towards this, he with the help of some like-minded friends, set up a fund to aid writers. The first works by Kuvempu, Bendre and Shivarama Karanth were brought out with support from this fund. All three of them, who were still finding their feet in the early thirties, went on to receive the Jnanpith Award years before Masti!

Innumerable instances of Masti having helped people in need have been recorded. His concern for the self-respect and worth of the individuals is perhaps best illustrated in the case of GP Rajaratnam, one of the important writers of the Navodaya period. Rajaratnam had a Master's degree in Kannada but was unemployed. Masti was then

Commissioner for Census. Rajaratnam asked for a clerk's job in the latter's office. Instead Masti offered Rajaratnam a stipend equal to the salary he would have received, and commissioned him to translate into Kannada, two of the books which he admired. This is how we have the travelogues of Huien Tsang and Fa-hien in Kannada.

What Masti did with the Jnanpith Award money is of a piece with what he had practised all through his life. While one-third of the money was earmarked for the publishing of his own works, the rest was to be used by the Masti Trust to award prizes for the best short story collections every year.

That Masti was a colossus of twentieth century Kannada literature is evident from the numerous books he had to his credit – over one hundred and twenty, some of them in English. Like most writers of the Navodaya tradition, Masti used all literary forms for his creative expression. But his reputation as a short story writer has tended to obscure his contribution to poetry, drama, criticism and journalism. A brief look into his achievements in these areas is in order before moving on to consider his forte, the short story.

PROSE: Non-fiction

Bhava, a kind of an autobiography, written when he was almost eighty, is Masti's most ambitious work. Though it lists the main events of his life in a chronological order, it is more a narration of his attitude to his own life at various stages, and is a mine of information on the ambience which made Masti. As in his writing, one is aware of the total control Masti has over his emotions throughout his life. Two things stand out very clearly. One, that his inner life seems to have had no great upheavals at any stage. The other, that his unquestioning faith in God stayed with him till the end. Reading the first part, which deals with the first three decades of his life, is a great experience. We find ourselves relating his descriptions of the villages of his boyhood with those that we see in his most successful stories, and are impressed by his ability to create a scene and breathe life into it.

The editorials that Masti wrote in *Jeevana* are a pleasure to read for the language, if not for anything else. Magazines like *Jeevana* were thin on the ground at that time. Hence the editorials, which a liberal mind like Masti wrote, must have greatly influenced the thinking of the educated middle class. In them, too, we see a civilized being, not of any particular political persuasion, take up the burning issues of the day.

The third area of his non-fictional writing is in the field of criticism. Masti wrote his criticism at a time when there was very little by way of creative writing. Masti, and some of his fellow writers were trying to change the taste of the reader. If we find he was not very rigorous in his assessment of any particular work, it was because the language of criticism was still in its infancy, some of the concepts which critics employed had come from the study of English literature, and there was a conscious attempt to place them against the backdrop of classical Indian and Sanskrit-based poetics. But more than anything else, the avowed purpose of the critic was to create enthusiasm in the reader for the book, so he deliberately ignored its deficiencies, if any. Masti's liberal thinking and his abhorrence of any kind of impassioned expression of opinions were responsible for the restraint with which he dealt with the works he took up for consideration.

The most distinctive work Masti left behind in the field of criticism is his *Adikavi Valmiki*, published in 1939. After having decided on what could be accepted as the authentic, Original version of the Ramayana, Masti proceeds to give us his version. His analysis of characters is full of compassion and is an expression of his liberal attitude towards what others might consider adharma.

In *Bharatateertha*, which deals with the Mahabharata, however, Masti's critical approach is overwhelmed by his pious attitude.

POETRY

Masti must have been writing poems even as he wrote his first stories, for his first collection of short stories and his first collection of poems, *Binnaha*, were published within a year or so of each other. It is interesting to note that this collection appeared a few years before the publication of English *Geethagalu*, BM Srikantia's translations of sixty poems from the English Romantic poets. Masti's volume was destined to have a far-reaching influence on Kannada literature, especially poetry, over the next three decades.

Masti came out with *Aruna* in 1924. Here, for the first time he uses what came to be known later as Blank Verse, for narrative purposes. *Madalingana Kanive* which appears in this collection, is one of his very successful narrative poems. His fondness for telling a story in verse – an obvious weakness in one who was born a master story-teller, stayed with him throughout his life. Navaratri, which came out in five parts between 1944 and 1953, contains nineteen stories narrated by different characters.

His most ambitious attempt in this genre was *SriRama Pattabhisheka*, published in 1972. Here, Masti tells Rama's story through the various characters associated with Rama, describing the events after the fact. The narration actually starts on the eve of Rama's coronation and goes over the events of the previous years in a panoramic sweep. It is interesting to note that Masti has introduced quite a few changes into Valmiki's *Ramayana* in building the story. Miracles, which hint at a super-human power at work, are missing in his telling. The poet attempts to present characters like Sita, Rama and Hanumantha as ordinary human beings who attained super-human status in their lives.

Masti was among the first Kannada poets to make extensive use of the sonnet form. *Malara*, a collection of eighty-two sonnets, published in 1933 is remarkable for the thematic variety of the sonnets and for the utter simplicity of their diction.

More classical than romantic, Masti's poetry does not sweep the reader off his feet. Though the poet gives repeated expression to his faith in man's inherent goodness and nobility, we have neither the flights of fancy nor the intensity of emotion that are typical of romantic poetry. The most characteristic feature of Masti's poetry is the even tone he adopts in unravelling the pattern that informs man's life. As Gopalakrishna Adiga says, "Masti's vision is not that of either Puttappa or Bendre, whose poetry may be said to have a certain metaphysical dimension to it. He does not lose himself in things which are alien to his nature. On the other hand, his poetry is the utterance of a contemplative man with total self-knowledge, who is interested in working out a modus operandi for relating to others ... There is no attempt here to tackle things which are beyond the poet's reach. One may feel like saying that such poetry lacks depth, but no one can say that it is false."

DRAMA

Masti wrote sixteen plays, most of them between the years 1923 and 1938. Two of them, *Yashodhara*, a verse play, and *Kakanakote*, are remarkable in that they create two worlds into which the reader or spectator is drawn. As in his poetry, there is no portrayal of any great conflict in *Yashodhara*. What action there is in the play is in the passage of the main character from a feeling of betrayal by the Buddha, to the ultimate state of peace and acceptance of life. Masti sets up a scene in which *Yashodhara* confronts the Buddha with her bitterness about his having deserted her. She even questions the rightness of some of the views and actions of the Master. What communicates itself most forcefully through the scene is the worldview of the playwright and the sympathy he had for the Indian woman – an attitude which informs most of his short stories and narrative poems as well.

Kakanakote is an entirely different proposition. It holds one spellbound because it is excellent theatre. An undercurrent of sadness coexists with humour throughout the play, which has the serious purpose of pitting the simple, life-loving and noble Kadu Kurubas against the power-wielders, whose lives are rife with deceit and intrigue.

The other plays that Masti wrote do not have the same appeal.

What was said of his poetry holds good for his plays too. There is no cataclysmic upheaval resulting from fierce emotions colliding against one another, hence there is no suggestion of anything even remotely tragic, in either the Shakespearean or the Greek sense. A world-view shaped by his personal metaphysics, with its core of gentleness and acceptance, is reflected in his plays. There is no place in them for evil and no place for aspects of human behaviour which leave the spectator disturbed and puzzled.

NOVEL

Of the four novels Masti wrote, *Subbanna*, appeared in 1928 and *Sheshamma*, in 1976. The two historical novels *Chennabasavanayaka*, and *Chikaveera Rajendra* were published in 1949 and 1956. The maturity that Masti displays in portraying the characters in Subbanna, one of the earliest novels of the Navodaya period, is amazing. *Sheshamma* is remarkable for it is an expression of Masti's own world-view and philosophy. The central character is almost an archetype very dear to Masti – a woman who goes through the trials and tribulations in her life with fortitude, her strength deriving from her faith in God.

The two historical novels that Masti wrote are indeed of great importance. While most Kannada novels in this genre presented a highly romanticised picture of a glorious past, Masti chose to depict the two states of Bidanur and Kodagu on their way to perdition, as a result of their corrupt rulers. Masti the story-teller has brought all his powers of narration to fruition in these novels. His genius enables him to make the tragedy of individuals, the tragedy of a whole people.

Chikaveera Rajendra is remarkable for the way in which the incidents make it possible for the reader to interpret the behaviour of the various characters, not in terms, of Fate and God's will, but in terms of the wisdom we have gained from psychology. If Chikaveera Rajendra, who strikes us initially as Evil incarnate, succeeds in forcing us to sympathize With him, even as he gets the punishment he seems so richly to deserve, it is because Masti has made him human. The other aspect of the novel is that it goes beyond what appears to be a traditional conflict between Good and Evil with the expected victory of Good over Evil in the end. Though there are characters who represent both sides in this classical conflict, Masti seems to imply that there is no guarantee that Good will win, unless it is reinforced by a will for positive action.

At this point in time, we can afford to ignore the controversy that surrounded the appearance of these novels. Much water has flowed under the bridge since then and critics and writers have been unstinting in their praise of *Chikaveera Rajendra* as a novel of great merit. Lankesh, who researched the history of the Veerashaiva community to write his revolutionary play, Sankranti, has praised the undercurrent of sadness and lyricism of the novel and added that it has grown with him over the years, yielding a new Significance with each reading. Girish Kamad, who has also turned to the same source in history for his latest play, *Taledanda*, has called *Chikaveera Rajendra* a celebration of the variety and richness of human experience.

SHORT STORY

Masti began his career as a short story writer and his finest achievement is undoubtedly in that field.

God, who Masti believed created this world, and ran the lives of all the creatures that people it, must have been pleased with the world that Masti created. In it you have princes rubbing shoulders with paupers, kings with knaves, rishis with rascals – a staggering variety of characters. While most of them came from a society the writer was familiar with, several belong to the pages: of history and mythology. Many of his stories are based on the lives of remarkable people from other countries, and he gives fictional accounts of events which shaped them.

Masti left behind him one hundred stories written between 1910 and 1985. But his eminence as a writer of short stories is not because he was the first to write them. In fact he has acknowledged the contribution of Kerur Vasudevachar, Panje Mangesha Rao and MN Kamath who had written short stories before him. Masti's greatness lies in that he was the first to make use of the form in such a distinctive manner, to present his unique world-view.

Looking back, it is possible to note one aspect of his art which is of considerable importance. He chose characters, who were ordinary human beings and created events around them which brought out their gentleness, their compassion and the nobility of their souls. A city-educated young man who is swept off his feet by the charms of a girl in his village ("Ranga's Marriage"), a hapless and harassed primary school teacher ("Our Teacher"), a young barber who falls in love with an acrobat ("Venkatashami's Love Affair"), a shrewd but lovable curd-seller ("Mangamma, the Curd-seller") and a jogi who is falsely accused of stealing a chicken ("Jogyora Anjappa's Chicken"), characters like this abound in his earlier stories. There is an inner strength in them which enables them to surmount the difficulties they encounter and accept the suffering which follows, without losing their essential humanity. The appeal of the stories derives from the implied suggestion that it does not take much for an ordinary human being to raise himself to a higher level of existence, thus filling the reader with hope for himself as an individual and for humanity as a whole.

We find a subtle shift in the thematic content of the stories of his later years. Most of them are used more or less as vehicles to communicate the writer's worldview. The characters too are frequently borrowed from history or mythology. The writing, however, continues to bear the distinctive Masti stamp.

It is remarkable that though Masti belonged to the Navodaya period, he did not surrender himself to the excesses, either of emotion or expression, that one normally associates with writers in the romantic mould. This is as true of his fiction as it is of his poetry. He was perhaps the only Kannada writer of the pre-Independence days who consciously used the language of the common man. It enabled him to achieve the impact that he desired without taking recourse to any kind of heightened expression. The matter-of-fact treatment of intensely emotional situations mark most of his successful stories. "Venkatashami's Love Affair" illustrates the effect he achieves through understatement.

Critics have drawn our attention to the technical device that Masti used, to gain a certain psychological distance between the writer and the events which go to make the story. He states at the outset, that he is narrating a story or an incident he had heard from somebody ("Venkatashami's Love Affair" and "An Unfortunate Woman"). This device, an essential element of the oral tradition suggests that Masti followed the traditional Indian way of telling a story. By using this technique, Masti the writer saved himself from getting involved in the narrative and the temptation of passionate expression. The measured tone that Masti adopts has its disadvantages. There is no scope for emotional peaks and valleys and it is not surprising if, after a while, the reader begins to long for them. Conflicting emotions are present, it is true, but the civilized tone suggests that the writer is on a proselytizing mission. One often finds him intruding into the narration with a direct statement of his world-view and it seems he has not been able to maintain the psychological distance between himself and the events in the story. Even his celebrated novel, Chikaveera Rajendra has passages which can be taken out without any loss to the narrative.

Masti was too great a writer not to know that a story should have an independent existence and that there is a logic which governs the feelings and actions of the characters he puts into it. No story can be true to itself if it is a mere vehicle of the writer's beliefs. The world-view held by the writer should be like a bonus which the reader receives after being thoroughly immersed in the tale and the telling of it. Mastl knew himself and the values he stood for. He firmly believed in God and His power over the destinies of the people He created. He believed in tradition and its capacity to sustain us even today. Acceptance of what Fate brings into our lives was at the centre of his philosophy. And Masti uses every opportunity the stories provide to state his conviction. But there are occasions when Masti the man is brushed aside by Masti the story writer. For example, the narrator at the end of one of his stories, *Velurina Lakshamma* says,

"Ramu is our youngest child. He doesn't know how to write. The only thing he knows is to scribble on the slate. When the slate is covered with lines, he asks me to look at what he has written. Writing for him is nothing but scribbling. If, with some luck, one of the lines turns out to be a letter, it's not his fault. Brahma's writing is no different. Unpredictability is its characteristic. Not even one in a thousand is good. And if one turns out to be good, it's not his fault.

"My wife was convinced that all this was Vedanta. She didn't pay any attention to it."

My father died over sixty years ago when I was only a child. It seems that Masti knew him. Though this gave me the desire to meet him and though I had seen him on many public occasions, it was only when I was twenty that I summoned enough courage to speak to him. That was in 1946. The year he made me a poet.

Those were the days of pain and despair when I was struggling to come out of an unfulfilled love affair. I had written what I thought was a poem, mostly as a therapeutic exercise, to exorcise the anguish that filled my heart. Though I was living with Prof MV Sitaramiah, a writer in Kannada, I did not have the courage to show him what I had written. I had not studied Kannada, even as a second language, and I had nursed a secret ambition to be a sensational writer in English. But I had to know whether the thing I had written was a Kannada poem. I sent it to *Jeevana*, of which Masti was the editor, and decided that if it ever got published there, I would write poetry.

It was not my passion for literature that made me pounce on the next six issues of the magazine as soon they hit the stands. The poem did get printed, after all, and I was a poet. The fact that it finds no place in my first collection of poems does not matter.

Masti had given my poem a place, he had raised me from the dead and given me a second birth.

When I visited him at his house, I am sure Masti thought that I had gone there to express my gratitude. He did not know that he had made me a much greater gift. I mentioned my father to him and said that he had run a monthly magazine, *Prabodhaka*, in Kannada, from Bombay till his death in 1932. Masti knew him and spoke warmly of the pioneering work that *Prabodhaka* had done. That brought us closer.

As I recall Masti now, nearly seven years after his death, I am convinced that the gods must have given him the gift of an inexhaustible chalice of love for all creatures, great and small. What stands out in my memory like an etching, is the single nama he wore on his forehead. And the way his eyes turned into mere slits as laughter burst out of him, to inundate the hundred furrows on his weathered face. Like most men over sixty in our blessed land, he too was prone to dispense words of advice. On occasion, he was intolerant of views which differed from his own and would not hesitate to admonish you, only to follow it up with a joke, and his unrestrained laughter. It took away the tension. At the end of the visit that is what one remembered – his laughter, his love of life and his genuine concern for the human condition.

Masti was once invited to give a lecture. The gentleman who introduced the guest spoke in English, with the usual and fashionable apology that he would commit innumerable mistakes if he spoke in Kannada. When it was Masti's turn to speak, he turned to the gentleman and said, "Sir, who would think of criticizing you for committing mistakes when you speak Kannada? The mistakes you made when you spoke in English could have been made in Kannada too."

Later, when I asked him whether he had indeed made such a remark, he burst into a child's laughter and said, "What do you think, sir? Would I do such a thing?"

I am sure he would. There was a mischievous imp in him till his dying day.

I have referred to Masti's occasional intolerance. But he was only being human on those occasions. He was pleased when his writing was praised and hurt when his work was censured. Mention has been made of the anguish he felt when there was a controversy about his historical novels. He was upset when a reputable critic remarked that Masti had no genuine sense of Evil. He was puzzled by Gopalakrishna Adiga's poem which was a reaction to his comment that a poet should write so common people could understand him. He sincerely wanted me to believe in God and was hurt when I maintained that belief in God was not necessary to lead a moral life.

I remember the moment in the interview when our discussion took a theological turn. I felicitated Masti on his having lived for ninety three years. He came back with the reply that he was certain God had a purpose in keeping him on earth for all those years. I said I had great regard for him and people like him, who had an unshakeable faith in the existence of God, but that I was incapable of such total surrender. Ours was an age when a man had to learn to live with his doubts – doubts about God, about tradition, I added. I remember so vividly, the sound of his spontaneous laughter stopping me mid-sentence. His disarming response was, "Do you know, sir, it is God who has planted such doubts in you? That is His way of putting you to the test." I had no answer to that.

Again during the interview, we found ourselves discussing the relationship between literature and society. He granted that the influence of religion was generally on the wane. "We used to get our hridaya samskara from religion, but we cannot depend on it to the same extent as we did in the past. We need an alternate source which we can tap for it. And that source is literature," he said. If there was sadness as he spoke of the decline of religion and its influence on the conduct of man, there was hope when he asserted that literature, and art in general, could provide the same strength.

There was passion in his voice when he referred to the role that tradition plays in guiding man. I listened to him, not convinced that our great tradition had answers to the complex problems of the present day. Suddenly, I realised that I was in the presence of one of the noblest examples this tradition had produced.

Arms round your shoulder when you ran into him on the street ... a blouse piece and coconut for your wife ... an autographed copy of his latest book when you visited his home ... the pockets of his ever-present coat bulging with sweets for the children he came across on his way to the Gandhi Bazaar Club, a place he visited as regularly as any devout contemporary of his would, a temple.

That was Masti Venkatesha Iyengar, one of the finest conservatives, through whom our tradition expressed its timeless relevance.

"When Death strikes
learnt words are the first to die
and meaning lies like flotsam
on a stretch of sand ...

Lines from one of my poems written a few years ago. If words did not die in me when Masti died, it was perhaps because his passing was more a fulfillment than an end. It was a gestalt, a completion of a circle suggesting fruition and ripeness, not just a fail.

I remember thinking of the club, and the trees on Krishna Rajendra Road where it is situated, when I heard of his death. The tail trees that lined the road and kissed the clouds thirty years ago when Masti walked along, are no longer there. There are frail-looking saplings instead. When he went to the club, Masti must have seen in them the dream to grow taillike the trees he knew in his prime. He must have been pleased that the play would go on. That there would be no final act to the play.

It has been a richly rewarding experience, translating some of Masti's short stories for this book. I am grateful to Katha for having asked me to undertake the task.

February, 1993 Ramachandra Sharma

A time for reflection

Ranga's Marriage

When you see this title, some of you may ask, "Ranga's Marriage?" Why not "Ranganatha Vivaha" or "Ranganatha Vijaya?" Well, yes. I know I could have used some other mouth-filling one like "Jagannatha Vijaya" or "Girija Kalyana." But then, this is not about Jagannatha's victory or Girija's wedding. It's about our own Ranga's marriage and hence no fancy

title. Hosahalli is our village. You must have heard of it. No? What a pity! But it is not your fault. There is no mention of it in any geography book. Those sahibs in England, writing in English, probably do not know that such a place exists, and so make no mention of it. Our own people too forget about it. You know how it is – they are like a flock of sheep. One sheep walks into a pit, the rest blindly follow it. When both the sahibs in England and our own geographers have not referred to it, you can not expect the poor cartographer to remember to put it on the map, can you? And so there is not even the shadow of our village on any map.

Sorry, I started somewhere and then went off in another direction. If the state of Mysore is to Bharatavarsha what the sweet karigadabu is to a festive meal, then Hosahalli is to Mysore State what the filling is to the karigadabu. What I have said is absolutely true, believe me. I will not object to your questioning it but I will stick to my opinion. I am not the only one who speaks glowingly of Hosahalli. We have a doctor in our place. His name is Gundabhatta. He agrees with me. He has been to quite a few places. No, not England. If anyone asks him whether he has been there, he says, "No, annayya, I have left that to you. Running around like a flea-pestered dog, is not for me. I have seen a few places in my time, though." As a matter of fact, he has seen many.

We have some mango trees in our village. Come visit us, and I will give you a raw mango from one of them. Do not eat it. Just take a bite. The sourness is sure to go straight to your brahmarandhra. I once took one such fruit home and a chutney was made out of it. All of us ate it. The cough we suffered from, after that! It was when I went for the cough medicine, that the doctor told me about the special quality of the fruit.

Just as the mango is special, so is everything else around our village. We have a creeper growing in the ever-so-fine water of the village pond. Its flowers are a feast to behold. Get two leaves from the creeper when you go to the pond for your bath, and you will not have to worry about not having leaves on which to serve the afternoon meal. You will say I am rambling. It is always like that when the subject of our village comes up. But enough. If anyone of you would like to visit us, drop me a line. I will let you know where Hosahalli is and what things are like here. The best way of getting to know a place is to visit it, don't you agree?

What I am going to tell you is something that happened ten years ago. We did not have many people who knew English, then. Our village accountant was the first one who had: enough courage to send his son to Bangalore, to study. It is different now. There are many who know English. During the holidays, you come across them on every street, talking in English. Those days, we did not speak in English, nor did we bring in English words while talking in Karmada. What has happened is disgraceful, believe me. The other day, I was in Rama Rao's house when they bought a bundle of firewood. Rama Rao's son came out to pay for it. He asked the woman, "How much should I give you?" "Four pice," she said. The boy told her he did not have any "change," and asked her to come the next morning. The poor woman did not understand the English word "change" and went away muttering to herself. I too did not know. Later, when I went to Ranga's house and asked him, I understood what it meant.

This priceless commodity, the English language, was not so widespread in our village a decade ago. That was why Ranga's homecoming was a great event. People rushed to his doorstep announcing, "The accountant's son has come," "The boy who had gone to Bangalore for his studies is here, it seems," and "Come, Ranga is here. Let's go and have a look."

Attracted by the crowd, I too went and stood in the courtyard and asked, "Why have all these people come? There's no performing monkey here."

A boy, a fellow without any brains, said, loud enough for everyone to hear, "What are you doing here, then?" A youngster, immature and without any manners. Thinking that all -these things were now of the past, I kept quiet.

Seeing so many people there, Ranga came out with a smile on his face. Had we all gone inside, the place would have turned into what people call the Black Hole of Calcutta. Thank God it did not. Everyone was surprised to see that Ranga was the same as he had been six months ago, when he had first left our village. An old lady who was near him, ran her hand over his chest, looked into his eyes and said, "The janewara is still there. He hasn't lost his caste." She went away soon after that. Ranga laughed.

Once they realised that Ranga still had the same hands, legs, eyes and nose, the crowd melted away, like a lump of sugar in a child's mouth. I continued to stand there. After everyone had gone, I asked, "How are you, Rangappa? Is everything well with you?" It was only then that Ranga noticed me. He came near me and did a namaskara respectfully, saying, "I am all right, with your blessings."

I must draw your attention to this aspect of Ranga's character. He knew when it would be to his advantage to talk to someone and rightly assessed people's worth. As for his namaskara to me, he did not do it like any present-day boy – with his head up towards the sun, standing stiff like a pole without joints, jerking his body as if it was either a hand or a walking stick. Nor did he merely fold his hands. He bent low to touch my feet. "May you get married soon," I said, blessing him. After exchanging a few pleasantries, I left.

That afternoon, when I was resting, Ranga came to my house with a couple of oranges in his hand. A generous, considerate fellow. It would be a fine thing to have him marry, settle down and be of service to society, I thought.

For a while we talked about this and that. Then I came to the point. "Rangappa, when do you plan to get married?"

"I am not going to get married now," he said.

"Why not?"

"I need to find the right girl. I know an officer who got married only six months ago. He is about thirty and his wife is twenty -five, I am told. They will be able to talk lovingly to each other. Let's say I married a very young girl. She may take my words spoken in love as words spoken in anger. Recently, a troupe in Bangalore staged the play Shakuntala. There is no question of Dushyantha falling in love with Shakuntala if she were young, like the present-day brides, is there? What would have happened to Kalidasa's play? If one gets married, it should be to a girl who is mature. Otherwise, one should remain a bachelor. That's why I am not marrying now."

"Is there any other reason?"

"A man should marry a girl he admires. What we have now are arranged marriages. How can one admire a girl with milk stains on one side of her face and wetness on the other, or so young that she doesn't even know how to bite her fingers?"

"One a neem fruit, the other, a bittergourd."

"Exactly!" Ranga said, laughing.

I was distressed that the boy who I thought would make a good husband, had decided to remain a bachelor. After chatting for a little longer, Ranga left. I made up my mind right then, that I would get him married.

Rama Rao's niece, a pretty girl of eleven, had come to stay with him. She was from a big town, so she knew how to play the veena and the harmonium. She also had a sweet voice. Both her parents had died, and her uncle had brought her home. Ranga was just the boy for her, and she, the most suitable bride for him.

Since I was a frequent visitor to Rama Rao's place, the girl was quite free with me. I completely forgot to mention her name! Ratna, it was. The very next morning I went to their house and told Rama Rao's wife, "I'll send some buttermilk for you. Ask Ratna to fetch it."

Ratna came. It was a Friday, so she was wearing a grand saree. I told her to sit in my room and requested her to sing a song. I sent for Ranga. While she was singing the song, ... *Krishnamurthy, in front of my eyes* ... Ranga reached the door. He stopped at the threshold. He did not want the singing to stop, but was curious to see the singer. Carefully, he peeped in. The light coming into the room was blocked. Ratna looked up and seeing a stranger there, abruptly stopped.

Suppose you buy the best quality mango. You eat it slowly, savouring its peel, before biting into the juicy flesh. You do not want to waste any part of it. Before you take another bite, the fruit slips out of your hand and falls to the ground. How do you feel? Ranga's face showed the same disappointment when the singing stopped.

"You sent for me?" he asked as he came in and sat on a chair. Ratna stood at a distance, her head lowered. Ranga repeatedly glanced at her. Once, our eyes met, and he looked very embarrassed. No one spoke for a long while.

"It was my coming in that stopped the singing. Let me leave." Words, mere words! The fellow said he would leave but did not make a move. How can one expect words to match actions in these days of kaliyuga?

Ratna ran inside, overcome by shyness.

After a while, Ranga asked, "Who is that girl, swami?"

"Who's that inside?" the lion wanted to know. The he-goat who had taken shelter in the temple replied, "Does it matter who I am? I am a poor animal who has already eaten nine lions. I have vowed to eat one more. Tell me, are you male or female?" The lion fled the place in fear, it seems.

Like the he-goat, I said, "What does it matter to either of us who she is? I'm already married and you aren't the marrying kind."

Very hopefully, he asked, "She isn't married, then?" His voice did not betray his excitement but I knew it was there.

"She was married a year ago."

His face shrivelled like a roasted brinjal. After a while, Ranga left, saying, "I must go. I have work at home."

I went to our Shastri the next morning and told him, "Keep everything ready to read the stars. I'll come later." I tutored him in all that I wanted him to say.

I found no change in Ranga when I met him that afternoon. "What's the matter? You seem to be lost in thought," I said.

"Nothing, nothing's wrong, believe me."

"Headache? Come, let's go and see a doctor."

"I have no headache. I'm my usual self."

"I went through the same thing when the process of choosing a girl for me was going on. But I don't think that that could be a reason for your present condition."

Ranga stared at me.

"Come, let's go and see Shastri," I suggested. "We will find out whether Guru and Shani are favourable for you or not."

Ranga accompanied me without any protest. As soon as Shastri saw me, he exclaimed, "What a surprise, Shyama! Haven't seen you for a long time."

Shyama is none other than your servant, the narrator of this tale.

I got angry and shouted, "What? Only this morning ..." Shastri completed my sentence, "You finished all your work and are now free to visit me." Had he not done so, I would have ruined our plan by bursting like grains that are kept in the sun to dry. I was extremely careful of what I said afterwards.

Shastri turned to Ranga. "When did the young son of our accountant clerk come home? What can I do for him? It's very rarely that he visits us."

"Take out your paraphernalia. Our Rangappa seems to have something on his mind. Can you tell us what's worrying him? Shall we put your science of astrology to the test?"

There was authority in my voice as I spoke to Shastri. He took out two sheets of paper, some cowries and a book of palmyra leaves, saying, "Ours is an ancient science, ayya. There's a story to it ... But I won't tell you that story now. This is not a harikatha which allows you to tell a story within a story ... You may get bored. I'll tell it to you some other time."

Shastri moved his lips fast as he counted on his fingers and then asked, "What's your star?" Ranga didn't know. "Never mind," Shastri indicated with a shake of his head. He did some more calculations before saying in a serious tone, "It's about a girl."

I had been controlling my laughter all this while. But now I burst out laughing. I turned to Ranga. "Exactly what I had said!"

"Who is the girl?" It was your humble servant who asked the question.

Shastri thought for a while before replying, "She probably has the name of something found in the ocean."

"Kamala?"

"May be."

"Could it be Pachchi, moss?"

"Must it be moss if it's not kamala? Why not pearl or ratna, the precious stone?"

"Ratna? The girl in Rama Rao's house is Ratna. Tell me, is there any chance of our negotiations bearing fruit?"

"Definitely," he said, after thinking for some time.

There was surprise on Ranga's face. And some happiness. I noticed it.

"But that girl is married ..." I said. Then I turned to him. His face had fallen.

"I don't know all that. There may be some other girl who is suitable. I only told you what our shastra indicated," Shastri said.

We left the place. On the way, we passed by Rama Rao's house. Ratna was standing at the door. I went in alone and came out a minute later.

"Surprising. This girl isn't married, it seems. Someone told me the other day that she was. What Shastri told us has turned out to be true after all! But Rangappa, I can't believe that you have been thinking of her. Swear on the name of Madhavacharya and tell me, is it true what Shastri said?"

I do not know whether anyone else would have been direct. Ranga admitted, "There's greater truth in that shastra than we imagine. What he said is absolutely true."

Shastri was at the well when I went there that evening. I said, "So Shastrigale, you repeated everything I had taught you without giving rise to any suspicion. What a marvellous shastra yours is!" He didn't like it at all.

"What are you saying? What you said to me was what I could have found out myself from the shastras. Don't forget, I developed on the hints you had given me."

Tell me, is this what a decent man says?

Rangappa had come the other day to invite me for dinner. "What's the occasion?" I asked.

"It's Shyama's birthday. He is three."

"It's not a nice name – Shyama," I said. "I'm like a dark piece of oil-cake. Why did you have to give that golden child of yours such a name? What a childish couple you are, Ratna and you! I know, I know, it is the English custom of naming the child after someone you like ... Your wife is eight months pregnant now.

Who's there to help your mother to cook?"

"My sister has come with her."

I went there for dinner. Shyama rushed to me when I walked in and put his arms round my legs. I kissed him on his cheek and placed a ring on his tiny little finger.

Allow me to take leave of you, readers. I am always here, ready to serve you.

You were not bored, I hope?

An Old Tale

It was the evening of a day close to Ashadha Pournima. The sun, tired after playing hide-and-seek with the clouds throughout the day, had moved towards the west. The clouds were scattered across the sky, looking frantically for some way to escape from the wind. The wind, having chased them, now gently, now spiritedly, like a shepherd boy herding his flock, had no

energy left and had turned into a light breeze. It moved through the huge trees by the riverside, bringing a sense of peace to everyone.

"It has only been a game all this while. Must do some work now," thought the sun. He managed to get out of the clutches of the clouds and looked around him. Then, he spread his sharp rays over the world, illuminating it with his splendour. The sun was serious about his work, the wind was quiet. Both were engrossed in their respective tasks. The grove on the bank of the river hummed with the primeval sound of the universe. The river, when it was but a trickle, had played with all the pebbles it met on its way – the big ones and the little ones. Now that it had attained maturity, it had acquired a dignity of its own. Then, too, it had flowed towards the sea. But it was not obsessed with its journey. Now, it was only conscious of its duty. But even if it had the status of an adult, should there not be a little playfulness too? So, it went round and round in some places, jumped and danced in others, making soft sounds as it flowed along.

The rays of the sun touched the river, the grove on its banks, the quiet village in the distance. They reached out to the villagers, the cattle returning home, heavy with milk, the calves calling out for their mothers, and bathed everything in a golden glow. The sun realised that the world had its radiance from him. He saw it all and he wanted to stay. But he had to go. Faced with this dilemma, the sun went down. The day ended. A calm filled the earth.

Watching all this, and taking in the peace and happiness which pervaded the place, was a sanyasi, seated on a durbhasana, in the middle of a math by the riverside. He was not very old. Forty-five or so may be. The vibhuti-smeared forehead and the glow on his face made it resemble the ash-covered embers in the angishthi beside him. An ochre-coloured robe was wrapped around him.

Now that the frolic of the sun and wind had ended, there was a stillness everywhere. It is probably the same for most people. But the sansyasi, there had never been any playfulness. Even as a child, this son of a brahmin had shown signs of a keen intellect. So at a very young age, he had been accepted into the ashrama by his guru, who taught him the Ashtangayoga and trained him to become a disciple worthy of his teacher. As a result, he only knew the duties of an adult, but had no opportunity to learn anything about play, which is the duty of a child. After the guru, he was appointed the head of the math. He believed that it was the bounden duty of a disciple to follow the guidelines laid down by his noble guru, and do nothing that would bring dish on our to the guru's name. Having led such a life, he had attained true peace. Only those whose lives are pure and unblemished can attain it without much difficulty. The sanyasi was now enjoying the fruit of his principled existence. As he was sitting there, in complete harmony, physically and spiritually, with his tranquil surroundings, a disciple came from inside the math and said, "Swami, I have corrected all the copies."

"Good."

In his contemplation of the beauty of nature, the sanyasi had forgotten everything else. But now his mind returned to the thought that had been worrying him since the afternoon.

It was not a part of the sanyasi's routine to reflect upon his actions. But on that day, something unusual had happened. He had, as on any other day, finished his puja of the Goddess Sharada, eaten his Simple meal and taken a class with all his disciples. Then followed the lesson for Shesha.

The sanyasi had been looking for a very bright young brahmachari whom he could train to take over from himself and who would meet With his own guru's approval. He had found Shesha, brought him to the math and started teaching him separately, after the lessons for the others were over. That afternoon Shesha sat before the guru with a book in his hand. Usually, the disciple read a shloka and the commentary on it. Sometimes the guru would offer his comments. On that particular occasion, Shesha read this sentence from the book, A woman's beauty is sure to attract every man, be he old, or wise or a sanyasi.

Hearing it, the guru thought to himself, So we have come to this shloka! Vyasa's words. He must have lost his heart many a time. He was old, yes, and he was wise. But what did he know about a sanyasi? He said to Shesha, "Wait. Correct that sentence. Say – A woman's beauty is sure to attract the old man and the wise man. But never a sanyasi."

Shesha was scared. He mumbled, "Swami, Vyasa's words ..."

The guru cut him short. "You do not know it, but remember, a man may speak about what he knows, not about that which he knows nothing of Vyasa knew nothing about sanyasis." The disciple made the correction. "Make the change in all the copies in the library," the Guru instructed him and ended the lesson for the day.

This is what the disciple had come to tell the guru that evening – that he had made the change. The guru had spent the entire afternoon wondering whether his decision to change Vyasa's text was right or not. When he heard the disciple's words, the same question returned to his mind. No matter how much he thought over it, he did not think he had done anything wrong.

It could not have been his experience alone. His own guru also must have gone through a similar one. He remembered how, when he was a disciple, he had come to that particular shloka, while reading the book aloud in his guru's presence. His voice had dropped in embarrassment. When there was no comment from the guru, he had stopped. The guru had told him to continue. At the end of the lesson, he had asked his guru, "Why has Vyasa made such a statement?" His guru had replied, "It is not wrong. One may say that a woman's birth is inferior to a man's, but there is no doubt that a woman's soul is more refined than his. It is natural for that which is inferior to be drawn towards what is superior. This is what attraction means. An iron filing turns towards a magnet. It doesn't matter whether the iron is pure or impure. A woman is like a magnet, the man, like the iron filing. Even the most superior of men turns towards her. It is possible that such an attraction is an entirely blameless one." The sanyasi's intellect may have found this interpretation acceptable, but his heart did not. Rather dissatisfied, he had let the matter lie. He took the guru's words to mean that he, the guru, had never lost his heart to a woman. He was certain that the guru's soul was pure.

When the guru had given up his hallowed body by going into a samadhi, the sanyasi had become the head of the math. There was nothing in his life, either, that he needed to be ashamed of. Never had a woman's beauty moved him. From his childhood and until now, he had come across many women. First, his own mother, the very embodiment of both beauty and dignity. He saw the same qualities in the image of Sharadambe, whom he worshipped every day. His mother was very beautiful and so were his four sisters. All of them had had children, and were dead now. He had seen their beauty too.

Once, when he was still young, some enthusiastic disciples had arranged for some young prostitutes to walk in front of his palanquin during a procession. Like everybody, they too had looked at him. They made some seductive gestures. But he had had no eye for them. Surprised by his indifference, the girls had turned their attention to the others. Later, when he understood the was of the world, he ordered that prostitutes should not parade like that in any procession. Some of the girls were extremely beautiful. Yet, he had remained unmoved.

Even now, as he walked along the river-bank, he would sometimes see the village women bathing in the river. On seeing him, the younger ones would rearrange their clothes in embarrassment or hide themselves in the water. The sanyasi would look the other way and walk on. He used to think that the gopis must have wantonly flirted like this with our Krishna and made him take their sarees and climb up a tree. This does not mean that the sanyasi had no eye whatsoever for a woman's beauty. Indeed, he found the female form pleasing. But he was not disturbed by it. He responded to beauty in any form, be it of a girl or a young woman, a boy or a youth. He often told himself, The Creator has been steadily increasing the quantum of beauty in His creation. It is His strategy to ensure that it lasts for ever. The sight of a full-bodied street cow with wide eyes, its small, sensitive ears, cocked and twitching, the tiny reddish horns like the new-born shoots of a banana tree, gave him the same pleasure as that of a comely girl. Many beautiful women would gather in the houses of his worthy disciples when he went to receive alms. Dressed in attractive sarees and blouses and decked in jewels, they would coyly lower their heads knowing that all the men were looking at them. Their shyness made them look even prettier. With eyes sparkling more brightly than the diamonds they wore, they would approach him to touch his feet, which rested on the clean floor – feet that had become dark and dry because of the strict discipline to which he had subjected his body. It would remind him of the image of a dry twig that had been carried by the flowing water and left beside a lotus stem, that swayed gracefully to the gentle breeze, in the pond opposite the math. He had not lost his heart to female beauty, even though he had seen it in all its extraordinariness and variety.

Each day, while performing the puja to the goddess Sharada, the mother of the world, he would contemplate her quiet beauty. If it could be enhanced, at all, it was only by a firm understanding of the secret of creation. He would lose himself in contemplation of her just as he had lost himself in the beauty of nature that evening. Was desire behind such contemplation? No. And that was why he was a little unhappy with Vyasa's statement. Why should a pure mind not react to those words? 'There was nothing wrong in what he had done that afternoon, the sanyasi thought. A touch of vanity too must have crept into his mind. When there was so much goodness, why should there not be some pride too?

Half seriously, half jokingly, he had thought, Why should Vyasa, who had all the attributes of any man with a family, talk about sanyasis? A smile of satisfaction spread over his face, for he felt confident that even if he underwent the most rigorous examination, in the sharpest light of the all-seeing sun, no flaw would be seen in him.

Certain essential elements had been left out of the sanyasi's self-examination. A feeling that pleases one's mind appears as the mind's response to the attractiveness of the thing perceived. Did his mind not wish that his asceticism was admired by the women bathing in the river, as he walked past without looking at them? Was it just that he was not tempted when he sawall those beautiful women in the houses of his disciples? Did he not feel like looking at a pretty face, a second time ? And even if he did, had his innermost desire to demonstrate his tremendous self-control prevented him from doing so? The sanyasi had not considered this possibility at all.

Of course he was pleased by the Sight of something beautiful. If his pride had not stood in the way, the feeling that gave him pleasure would have been identified as the object's appeal. It did not occur to the sanyasi that the uprightness of his conduct could have come from his pride, not dharma.

It was getting dark. The birds that gathered in the grove by the river fell silent, after they had let out their cacophonous calls believing that they had made divine music. Everything around was blurred as Mother Night came on silent feet and spread her pallu of sleep over all the world. The village lights twinkled among the trees. One could faintly hear a late-coming cow call for its calf as it approached the village. As these sounds subsided, one became aware of the river water hissing as it swirled around on its way. A disciple in the math was reciting shlokas. As the sanyasi sat there thinking and taking in the peace around, it started to drizzle.

Suddenly, the sound of an anklet was heard, as if someone was walking quickly towards the math. The sanyasi looked up wondering who it was. No one came to the math at that hour. The way to the math ran through a forest and there was a hill nearby where cheetahs were known to live, so people were afraid to take that path after nightfall. If it grew dark while they were on the way to the math, they would go to the village instead. But someone was coming there that evening. Must be a woman who had lost her way to the village and had wandered here, thought the sanyasi. He looked up, curious, as the jingling of the anklets came closer. A young woman stood at the door and called out, “Amma, is there anyone in the house?”

As it was almost dark, the sanyasi could not see her clearly. Everything was hazy in the dim light of the angishthi. She must have walked some distance in the rain. Her clothes were soaking wet.

“Who are you, amma?” he asked.

“Whose house is this, swami ? Yours?”

“This is God’s house, a math. Why do you ask?”

“Are there any women here?”

“No. But who are yell? Why have you come here?”

She came a little closer and seeing his ochre garments, asked, “Are you the swami of this place?”

“Yes, I'm the watchman.”

“Appa, I’m scared. I was much more scared when I heard that there were no women here. But I have got some of my courage back, now that I have seen you. It’s like finding my own father. You are a sanyasi. No one can say bad things about me, now. Ayyo! I don't know what happened to my husband. What shall I do?” The woman started crying.

The sanyasi felt sorry for her.

“Amma, what did you say happened to your husband? Did you come with him? From where?” he asked.

He was concerned about her, but at the same time he experienced a sense of exhilaration. Here was an opportunity to demonstrate that he was not tempted by a woman’s beauty. He had run his eyes over the wet saree which clung to her. Her apparent helplessness aroused an interest in her. And that was the sanyasi’s mistake.

The woman said, “Swami, my father’s house is in Ranganathapura. My husband and I came to Molleyooru on our way there. As we were walking along, he stopped and told me to carry on, saying that he would join me in a minute. He used to make fun of my slow pace, so I kept walking, to show him he was wrong. After I had walked some distance, I looked back to see how far behind he was. I couldn’t see him. I sat down to wait for him. He didn’t come for a long time, so I went back to the spot where he had stopped. There was no trace of him. I called out to him but he did not answer. I was frightened ... a woman, all alone. I remembered him saying that the path would lead to Molleyooru, so I started walking and reached this place. Appa, you must save my marriage. Send someone to look for my husband. I am very frightened.” She started crying again.

Her tears touched the heart of the sanyasi. He felt a great pity for her. “Amma, we have very few people here,” he said. “Whom shall I send to look for your husband? Don’t worry, no harm will come to him. You must have taken this turning at the point where the road divides into two. He must have taken the other one going towards the village, thinking you were heading there. That’s what must have happened. Stay here for the night. Tomorrow morning we will make enquiries in the village. You are sure to find that there is no reason to be anxious.”

“You are indeed like a father to me! But you say that there are no women here. How can I stay here all alone in the night?”

“Ammayya, you are like my own child. There is a room here. You can use it. I will sleep and keep watch. If something scares you during the night, call me. Don’t worry about anything.”

“You ... you are a sanyasi. I will do as you say. But send someone in the morning to look for my husband. Save my marriage, Appa.”

So saying, she prostrated before the sanyasi. Her tender fingers touched his feet.

It was the sanyasi’s habit to try to understand the full splendour of God by looking at the world around, which at best, expressed only half His beauty. Did he, in the same way, contemplate the beauty of the lady's form, which was only partially revealed by the wet saree? Who knows!

Or, like one's teeth which are reluctant to chew anything after having bitten into something extremely sour, had he exhausted all his reserve of courage in fighting Vyasa's statement, that he could not resist the touch of the lady's fingers? Whatever the reason, he felt a thrill pass through his body.

He was surprised by his own weakness. When she stood up, he called out for his disciples and asked them to bring some lamps. He was dazzled by the beauty their light revealed. Justas a traveller, caught unexpectedly in the Ashadha rains, looking up at the black clouds from the south-west, thinks that the rain will not stop, is suddenly dazzled by the lightning Indra etches with his Vajra on that darkness, and he blinks because he cannot bear the radiance, the sanyasi shut his eyes. As he looked at her, it seemed to him that Brahma had tried to explore all the possibilities of creating beauty out of curved patterns through the bow-shaped curls on her forehead, which ran all the way to her ears. He looked at her dark and arched eyebrows; at her eyelashes which seemed to be competing with each other to achieve the highest possible grace, while running a not-sa-straight race, having agreed to start from the same point, towards an identical destination; at her smooth round cheeks, the colour of lemon; at the check-patterned saree with gold lines that traced the curves and hollows of her sinuous body. The smile in her beautiful eyes seemed to say that she would not let it escape onto her lips until she set eyes on her lover, and so it had decided to come into her eyes instead. He noticed the dimple in her chin which looked like a screw Mother Nature had fastened to hold in place the grace which was spilling over; at the armlet and the bangles on her rounded wrists, at the nose-ring which was like a firefly near a champaka bud and at her black hair adorned with the white jasmine, contrasting with each other yet enhancing each other. The sanyasi was completely stunned by what he saw. Why did he have to set his eyes on her beauty that night, beauty that would knock a man off his feet and hold him prisoner?

Forgetting himself, he stared at her, utterly dazed.

Smiling slightly, she lowered her head and said, "Swami, why do I need this light? Just send someone with me. I'll go to the village."

The sanyasi was a little ashamed. "I got the lamp so that you could see your way into the room. Come, let's go in."

"I'll go to the village if someone accompanies me," she repeated.

"What is this talk of going to the village at this hour? I'm here to take care of you. Besides, you are in the presence of Sharada. You have no reason to fear anything. Come."

Everyone went inside. Someone gave her one of Sharadambe's old saris to wear. She participated in the puja, and ate a little of the food which had been prepared for the inmates. A mat was spread for her in a room next to the hall and an old piece of cloth, used in the service of Sharadambe, was given to her to cover herself with. The sanyasi told her that he would be sleeping outside and assured her once again, that she need have no fear. She smiled and said God was there to help her.

The sanyasi sat in meditation outside. A little later, the lady came out, did a namaskara to him and went back into the room. Shortly after, she came to the door again, cast a suspicious look at him and then shut the door and bolted it.

She was neither innocent nor worldly-wise. A young woman, very much like a kitten, whose play knows no guile. And that kitten had made a mouse of the sanyasi. He had never seen beauty like hers. For that matter, he had never looked at a beautiful object with desire. But on that night, he had made the mistake of wanting to find out what the essence of her attractiveness was. He had sensed that despite her obviously courteous behaviour, she was suspicious of him and thought it would be fun to give her a scare. This is how mischief is born, through contact. Move a broomstick in front of a cat, dull with sleep, if you like, and it is sure to get up and play, as if the broom is a mouse. Or, sit in front of a child and cover your eyes with your hand, saying that mother beat you. Or, place your hand near the child and cry out "Abba" as if you are hurt. The child is sure to turn away from whatever it was doing and remove your hand, or hit you, to justify your cry of pain. So far, the sanyasi had escaped being caught in the magic of a woman's charm. But now he was ensnared, like the child who wanted to make Teal, the adult's cry of pain. He wondered at his own foolishness and sat down to meditate. Usually, he saw nothing but the beauty of Sharadambe during his meditation. On that occasion, there was another image besides the gentle form of the goddess. Whose was it? It was that of the young woman. Never having known what play was, he found it reasonably easy to brush aside his desire for play. But now his mind knew desire, and it was still under its sway. He contemplated all that had taken place, and realised that he was bewitched by her. But what did that mean?

Did he want to have her for a wife? Cheh! What was this talk of a sanyasi marrying? Or, did he want her as a lover? No, such a vile thought would not enter his mind. What did he want, then? Only to look at her, go on looking at her. Nothing else. Just a Simple desire to see her again. Suppose you are walking along a street, and in someone's garden, you spot a rose bush with a beautiful red-and-white flower on it. You stop to look at it, to admire it. That does not mean that you intend to steal it, does it?

The sanyasi's desire was no different. He wanted to look at her again, more closely. But his training told him it was wrong, that he must conquer this overwhelming urge. So he called out to his disciple, Shesha. By the time Shesha came, the reason for which he had been summoned, had disappeared. "Bewitched by this girl's beauty, I am not sure what my mind will make me do. If Shesha is beside me, his presence might prevent me from behaving foolishly," the sanyasi had thought when he had called out to his disciple. But he had changed his mind by the time Shesha arrived. "I am not so evil, am I? My mind, which has been under my control till now, will not betray me today. If I don't have confidence in myself, how will Shesha's presence help me? Shall I forsake my faith in dharma and rely on my pride?" These, thoughts had convinced him that it was not necessary for Shesha to sleep near him.

The sanyasi himself was not clear what other thoughts ran through the innermost recesses of his mind. If Shesha were there with him, it would not have been possible for him to see that beautiful face again, no matter how intense the longing. He would have to suppress it. His desire was not unnatural. Also, he certainly had not meant any harm to her. All that he wanted was to look at her beautiful face and her enchanting form. Nothing more. He would not be able to gaze at her to his heart's content, in the morning. So he would wake her up during the night on some pretext or other and feast his eyes on her beauty. He would not be able to do it if Shesha were sleeping near him.

Perhaps he considered all this. The reason he changed his mind may have been his knowledge that it was pride, not dharma, which was at the base of his upright conduct. And an unconscious awareness that he would not be able to satisfy his desire if Shesha were beside him. So when the disciple came in response to his guru's call, the sanyasi just Said, "Nothing. Go and sleep."

So he threw away his pride and became helpless, like a cripple who is dependent on his walking stick, and yet throws it away, not appreciating its worth.

In his pure mind, desire kept growing, as time passed.

Suppose you are sitting on the bank of a clear pond one fine morning. You see the faint shadow of a cloud reflected in the water. The shadow is not an inherent property of the water, yet it makes the water look murky. As you are watching, suppose all the blackness of the shadow coagulates, and from it, emerges a dark, venomous water-snake. The dazzling beauty of the young woman had caused an unnatural shadow to appear in the pure waters of the sanyasi's mind. It had grown into a desire to see her beauty, like the snake emerging out of the water and sullying it.

He thought of the young woman's beauty again and again. He thought of the evening which glowed in response to the eternal peace all round, the darkness which gradually enveloped the world like the pallu of a saree with which a mother covers her baby before giving it her breast, the village lights which looked as if the god of Light had cut himself up into thousands of pieces and distributed them among the people thinking that it did not matter if he was reduced to fragments as long as he could serve the world. The jingling of the anklets had come like so many wavelets on the ocean of peace. The young woman's startling beauty which had forced him to shut his eyes when he saw it in the lamp-light. Her coyness, her suspicion, the fear and desire in her eyes and the indescribable playfulness which they suggested – he almost went insane with the longing to look at her. He felt like a fool. His attempts to divert his mind to the contemplation of the goddess Sharadambe were in vain. He was like one who repeatedly tells himself that he should not yield to hunger and thirst and wills his mind to turn away from thoughts of them. Yet those thoughts continue to assail his body in spite of his resolve to abjure them. The sanyasi's desire to look at her again assailed his mind in spite of his desire to fight it and grew with every passing moment. He could not contain it any longer.

You may wonder what was so special about her beauty. A woman's beauty is of two kinds. One has a gentleness about it which envelops one's soul. It is the beauty of motherhood. The other one is what invades the mind and casts a spell over it. That is the charm of the beloved .. Every woman is a mixture of both these and that is how a man's eyes see her. In most women, the two are more or less balanced. When a man perceives the beauty of mother-hood in a woman, it brings him peace, while the beauty of the beloved entrances him. A man whose mind is pure sees the beauty of motherhood in most women even if it is present in a small measure, and is blind to the other. What man can resist the other one, the beauty of the beloved, when it stands before his eyes as the very embodiment of grace and magic? Would any man, however chaste, survive such a test? He would certainly fail, just as the sanyasi had.

The sanyasi sat down for a little while. Then he decided that he would look at her once again, and went up to the door. He pushed it, but it was bolted from the inside. He put his ears to the door and listened to her even breathing, as she slept. How beautiful must her sleeping face be! He tried the door once again. There was a small sound. She got up with a start and asked anxiously, "Who's that?"

"It is me, amma" he said.

"Is it the swami of the math?"

"Yes."

"What's it, Appa? Has my husband come?"

"No. I just wanted to make sure you were sleeping."

"The comfort there is in sleep, is not there when one is awake, swami. I dreamt that I was on a journey with my husband."

"That is a good sign. You are no longer anxious, I hope?"

"No."

"What's this ? You have shut the door?"

"Yes, swami. I'm all alone, so to give myself courage, I closed it."

"Or because you have some doubts about me?"

"No, mahaswami."

"The door is still shut, even after this conversation?"

"You are a sanyasi. You may not appreciate what I'm saying. I'm alone here. What will people say if I were to let you in at this hour?"

"I'm a sartyasi. No one will say anything."

"I'm sure I am safe with you. But I have just woken up, my clothes are untidy, and it would not be right for you to see me in this state."

"You are not going to open the door, then?"

"No. I'll not open the door for any man other than my husband, whether he is wise or old or even a sanyasi."

The sanyasi was a little shaken. After a pause, he asked, "Do you know that shloka?"

"No. They are my own words."

"You are playing with me. You are so stem one moment and joking the next. Wait., I'll prove to you how ignorant the man who said it was. Open the door and you'll see that it is not true of a real sanyasi."

"You can say whatever you like. I will not open the door." "What if I push it open?"

"Do it and you'll learn a lesson."

The sanyasi waited for a while before he said, "I'm coming in," and pushed the door. It had not been bolted from the inside.

The lady was not to be seen anywhere. Instead, there was an old man with his hair tied on the top of his head, his face glowing with the power which comes from years of meditation.

The sanyasi was startled by what he saw on that face – a smile, and yet., it expressed a deep disapproval.

"You weren't attracted to her and yet you madly desired to see her face," the old man said.

The sanyasi fell at his feet., "I am a fool. Forgive me."

"You questioned the truth of what I had said. I can understand your doubts since you don't know me. But shouldn't you have faith in your own guru's words?"

"I am a great sinner."

"Fall at his feet then."

The sanyasi looked up. He saw his guru standing next to Vyasa. He prostrated at his feet.

When he got up to say something more, he found no one there except the woman. She was asleep. The sanyasi did not feel like looking at her. He knew that all this had happened due to his guru's grace. He shut the door as he went out. He sat down to meditate. Now he was able to fix his mind on Sharadambe.

It was morning once more and duty called. By the time the sanyasi came out of his meditation, everyone in the math was up and attending to their appointed chores. The young woman, accompanied by her husband who had come there earlier, looking for her, went to the sanyasi and did a namaskara to him.

"You saved my honour when there was no one to take care of me," she said.

"It was God who saved both you and me," the sanyasi replied. After a pause, he added, "I had come into your room last night."

"It must have been the confidence that I was under your protection, that made me sleep so soundly. I don't know anything about your having come in. I found the latch drawn in the morning, so I thought that I must have left it unlatched."

"You had bolted the door. I undid it."

The sanyasi insisted that the couple stay till the afternoon, told them to perform the puja to Sharadambe, and leave after having lunch. Not once was he drawn to her as he had been the previous evening.

That afternoon, while giving his usual lesson, the sanyasi told his disciple to restore the Original words of Vyasa's shloka.

"Did Sharadambe order you to restore it, mahaswami?" the disciple asked.

"Why do you ask?"

"I knew it when Sharadambe came here yesterday. But I didn't know what was in your mind. When you called me last night, I thought it was to let me have her darshana. Then you sent me away considering me unworthy of it. I didn't go back to bed but sat in the hall hoping you would call me again. I was aware that you spoke to her and opened the door, but then I must have fallen into a trance. When I came out of it in the morning, I knew that you had sent me away because I would not have been able to withstand the Sight of the goddess. That is why I asked whether it was Sharadambe who instructed you to restore the original text."

"The lady who went out just now, was she Sharadambe?"

"No. It was the one that came last night."

"What happened to her?"

"Mahaswami, how should I know? You have the power to work miracles. How can I comprehend what you do? You granted me the knowledge that it was Sharadambe who visited us. I know nothing else."

"Shesha, you are the wise one. And I? I am a fool. While your eyes saw Sharadambe, my eyes saw an ordinary woman. Listen."

The sanyasi narrated the events of the night to the disciple.

"Tell all the disciples in the math what happened to me, when a suitable opportunity offers itself. It is God who protects us as we walk the path of righteousness. Mere human effort is not enough. Pride destroys dharma, ayya. Is there a man who can claim that he is not tempted by beauty, when God has created it and invested it with His glory? It is a good thing that man is susceptible to temptation. He should, however, make sure that all his temptations are surrendered to God. It is He who confers power on things and it's only natural that man's mind is drawn to them. So man needs God's help to ensure that he is not led astray."

The sanyasi spent many years in the math. There was a bond of mutual affection between him and his disciple which only grew stronger as time passed. Many took to the path of dharma, owing to the greatness of the sanyasi who was honest about his mistake. The seat which he occupied and enriched by his presence is now a great and hallowed institution which has bestowed enlightenment, and the peace that follows from such wisdom, to hundreds of followers.

Our Teacher

It was Thursday. I was in a hurry as it was getting late for school. Lakshmi was behind me, almost running on her little feet. She was still asleep when I went to call her, and that had delayed things even more. As we walked along, we saw our teacher ahead of us. I slowed down too. There was no reason for us to rush when Teacher himself was taking it easy. That was

when Shastri, corning in the opposite direction, spotted him.

"So, Venkataramaniah, on your way to school?" he asked.

"Yes, swami, I am. Do you have a pinch of snuff?" Teacher asked.

"Here. What other news? Aren't you a little late?"

"What can I say, swami? My wife told me there was no salt in the house. I was late for school so I told her I couldn't get it. She started saying all kinds of things. Perhaps it would have been better if I had gone out and bought the salt. I would have reached the school by now. Problems, swami, problems ..."

"It's no problem. I'll send it to your house through one of the boys. Do you have the money for it? Give it to me."

Since Teacher was standing and talking, there was no point in our going on to school. So Lakshmi and I sat down to play Guchamma Nakshatra. We were so engrossed in our game that we did not notice our teacher had gone. I got up quickly saying, "Lakshmi, come, let's go. It's late. Teacher will be angry."

But Lakshmi just sat there, crying, because she had lost all her balapa sticks to me. I had not cheated. She lost them because she did not know how to play. I begged her to get up, but she kept wailing, "My sticks, my balapa sticks." I tried to reason with her. But she had no sense of fair play at all. She only knew that the chalk pieces were hers. Fed up with her crying, I gave back all the pieces I had won and tried to coax her into going with me. But she continued to stand there, asking for the chalk pieces. She would not listen when I told her I had given all her pieces back. "You have some more in your pocket," she said. Those are mine," I protested. It was no use. Finally, I handed her all the pieces I had. She would not have come to school otherwise. And I would not have had the excuse that I had gone to fetch Lakshmi, when Teacher asked me why I was late. I had won the game but she had won the chalk pieces! I was reminded of the occasion when the Inspector had come on a visit, and Saraswathi had got more marks than Gowri!

By the time we reached the school, Teacher had already started the lesson for the first standard. Lakshmi and I slipped in unnoticed and sat down.

After he finished with that class, he turned to our group and asked, "Why haven't Gowramma and Sitamma come as yet?"

"I came long ago, Teacher," I said.

"Good girl. Try to come earlier from now on, amma," he told me.

When he saw me nod my head in Lakshmi's direction, he added, "So you brought Lakshmi with you, did you? You are late every day because of her, I know. But come on time. Just for a few days more. The Inspector is going to visit the school any day so all of you should come on time and study properly. This is a new Inspector and he says he will present pearl necklaces to those who do well in studies. Saraswathamma, you must study hard, like Gowramma."

"Let her study well if she wants to. I don't have a squint, Saraswathi said.

Everyone laughed loudly. I did not want to, but I could not help joining them. Lakshmi clapped her hands and giggled. Naughty girl. Even Teacher wanted to laugh, but he controlled himself and scolded, "Cheh! You shouldn't say such things."

Saraswathi was proud that there was nothing wrong with her nose and eyes, and she made fun of Gowri's squint. There was nothing wrong with my nose and eyes either. Nor with Lakshmi's. Most people are like us. Yet Saraswathi was vain. It seems girls are like that. They think that a straight nose and proper eyes are all that they need. Their only desire is to please men. So whatever is required to do that, is enough for everything else. But even men are like that. Suppose there is a man who has passed his BA. He may be one-eyed, or have a dark complexion, or an ugly face. Yet he believes that all women achyire him because he has a degree. A man has to earn a living. If he has what is required to do that, then he thinks he is attractive to girls. Men do not realise that good looks do not come with education, and women do not know that you cannot pass an exam by beauty alone. A boy who is not good-looking thinks that education itself is good looks. Saraswathi, who was no scholar, thought that beauty was everything. After all, she had been praised by the Inspector the previous year, even though she had not learnt the lesson.

That was the day Gowri and Saraswathi, who were friends until then, fell out. The Inspector had asked the class what a river was. Saraswathi did not know. Only if you learn the lesson by heart you will know, won't you? She kept quiet. The Inspector turned to Gowramma, and she repeated, word for word, all that was written in Raghunatha Rao's book on geography. None of us felt jealous when Gowri got high marks. Gowri was a good student and we knew it. The Inspector asked another question. "How is a river formed?" Gowri did not know the answer. It was Saraswathi's turn. She replied, "The water that fans here and there, joins together to form a river." "Shabash!" exclaimed the Inspector. He turned to Teacher and complimented him for having prepared the girl so well. Teacher had actually coached Gowri. The Inspector had meant Saraswathi. Poor Teacher. Thinking the reference was to Gowri, he explained, "I have indeed worked very hard, mahaswami. You must have also noticed it. You can ask her for any detail in geography and she will tell you."

The Inspector realised that Teacher was talking about Gowri. "This girl? Yes. She has studied well, I know. But I was referring to the other one." Turning to Saraswathi, he asked, "What's your name, amma?"

"Saraswathibai."

"I was talking about Saraswathibai," said the Inspector.

"My rib-cage has gone dry trying to teach her," Teacher moaned.

It was the truth. As in the saying, You shall never learn and I shall never forget, Teacher was exhausted trying to teach Saraswathi. And she had managed to get a shabashgiri for saying something he had not taught her. Gowri was upset. From that day onwards the two girls were no longer friends. Gowri would taunt her, "Oho, your shabashgiriye! Such pride even without studying!" Saraswathi had only one reply, What can I do, tell me? I don't have your squint." Teacher was not aware of all this. He would advise Saraswathi to work hard like Gowri, and she would take that opportunity to humiliate Gowri.

But to return to that Thursday. After telling them not to say such rude things, Teacher assigned some work to the students. Every now and then someone in the class would remember what Saraswathi had said and start giggling. Or they would whisper among themselves. They munched the chakkali, mucchore and avalakki they had brought, and you could hear kutumkutum and gurumgurum sounds coming from them. They were busy doing everything but the work given. No one else had much interest in studying except Gowri who was sitting quietly, her brows knit together. Gowri had not forgotten her humiliation. While I waited for Teacher to ask us to submit our lessons, I was trying to cajole Lakshmi into giving my balapas back. My efforts were in vain. Before I could get really annoyed with her, there was another occasion for some mirth.

I do not know what Teacher was thinking about – something very practical, like what awaited him at home because he had left his household without salt., or about some metaphysical issue, or about *Rukku Samhite* – when a woman walked into the classroom. As soon as Teacher saw her in the doorway; he probably thought whatever was to take place at home, was about to happen here, in the school. Shaken out of his relaxed posture, he started to say something to her. But, in a slightly loud voice, his wife told him, "I told you that there was no salt in the house, yet you went straight to school. What do you expect me to do?"

"Should you come here just for that?" Teacher asked her.

"Whenever I ask for something, you take refuge in the school. And you issue an order that I should, under no circumstances, come here. What should I do, tell me. From now on, I will come to wherever you are, be it the school or anywhere else. And I will ask for things we don't have in the house. I can't stand this anymore."

"Couldn't you have borrowed some from the neighbours? If someone were to come here now and see you, what would happen to my reputation?"

"You will lose your reputation if somebody comes. What about the self-respect that I have to lose everyday? Rice from one house yesterday, dal from another one today, salt tomorrow. I'm fed up of having to borrow things. I am not going to ask anyone for anything any more. If you have money, buy it. Or say that you will bring it. But don't give me the excuse that you are late for school and run away. If you don't have any money, say so. We'll eat without salt."

In the meanwhile, there was a lot of excitement among the girls. Lakshmi had spotted Garudamari on the street. Garudamari?

Garudamari was a little kitten. Very pretty to look at. The girls used to wave a broomstick in front of it and the kitten would try to catch it, as if it was a mouse. They would pull its tail and make it spit in anger. They would share their snacks with it. The kitten was fond of us all, but liked Lakshmi more than anyone else. Once she had brought some tambittu. One was not sure whether her mother knew about it or not. Saraswathi, Gowri and I, along with all the others, surrounded her, and persuaded her to give us some of it. Unfortunately for us, Lakshmi had called the kitten and placed the tambittu in front of it for fun. The kitten, however, did not think it was a game. It picked up the tambittu and would not let go of it. It growled in protest if anyone went near it. Perhaps the kitten thought that it would get some tambittu from Lakshmi everyday, and so it showed special affection for her. Lakshmi did not mind losing her tambittu. She was proud that the kitten loved her and she would not leave it alone, petting and cuddling it all the time. Lakshmi had given it this name, Garudamari, because it was so pretty. Some parts of it were off-white, and the rest, pure white. Its neck looked a soft white while its nose and forehead were also white but with a few black patches.

Its mouth was red like the skin of a ripe papaya and the eyes were pure yellow like topaz. Its paws – only those who had been scratched, knew how sharp the nails were. That was our Garudamari.

When Lakshrni spotted the kitten, she ran after it and brought it back with her. A few girls joined us, as we made a circle around it, and played with it. I do not know what else Teacher and his wife talked about. Lost in our game, we did not notice what happened. Suddenly WP heard our teacher asking us to go back to our places. There was fear in his voice. Quickly we sat down – the kitten on Lakshmi's lap – and picked up our books.

When we looked up, we saw an elderly gendeman at the door, surveying us all with an air of absolute authority. He looked at our teacher standing near the table and asked, "Are you the teacher here?"

It was the Inspector. Only Inspectors talk to teachers in that tone. There is a marked difference between the way people talk to a teacher and the way an Inspector addresses him. Nobody should get upset because I say such things. I do not want my remarks to be taken seriously either. The authority an Inspector exercises over a teacher is like the courage a cat displays in catching a mouse.

Teacher too knew that it was the Inspector as soon as he heard the question. "Yes, mahaswami," he replied.

"Put on your turban. What do you mean being bare-headed?"

Our teacher knew the shastras and the Vedas. He could recite the *Raghuvamsha* and expound on philosophical matters. His heart was free from malice. I have recently come to know something about man's nature. Having watched my young children and seen how utterly pure and innocent their hearts are, I can say that our teacher had the heart of a child. Pure and guileless. He could not bear to see anyone suffering. That was why he often had no money for salt. There was no cunning whatsoever in him. Once he saw a cobra approaching a group of children, who were playing on the street. He knew the strictures against killing a cobra but he ignored them. He knew that if it attacked him, he was sure to die. But he put his fears aside and killed it. Even as the people who had gathered around praised this brahmin's courage, he took out his snuff box and placed a big-sized pinch of snuff on the head of the cobra. You probably know that there is a belief that a snake catcher puts a pinch of snuff in a snake's mouth when he catches it. The snuff makes the snake giddy and it falls senseless. Then he pulls out its fangs. Teacher had the same intention, perhaps. He did not seem to realise that a snake which was motionless enough to accept a pinch of snuff from him, would not know its taste either.

But even this courageous soul was terrified of two things. One was his wife. The other was the Inspector. When the latter thundered, "Put on your turban," Teacher was like a timid man at whom a live frog had been thrown. In his haste, he put on the turban, back to front. His face dripped with perspiration. I felt sorry for him, even though his appearance made me want to laugh.

The Inspector looked at Teacher, "Put your turban on the right way," he said sternly.

"Mahaswami!" said Teacher, taking it off and rearranging it.

But to his bad luck, it got completely undone. You cannot imagine the confusion that followed. The turban had come undone. The Inspector was furious. Not one girl in the class had learnt her lessons. Teacher was afraid he would lose his job if the Inspector began to ask the girls any questions. Moreover, there was his wife, sitting in the classroom. What would happen if the Inspector noticed her presence? What answer would he give, if the Inspector pointed to her and asked who she was? Teacher's mind was in a turmoil. I cannot describe his agony. You can only imagine it.

The Inspector looked at the teacher's wife. "Who is that? A teacher?"

Teacher, pretending to be busy tying the turban, mumbled, "Mahaswami?"

Who knows what the Inspector would have said at that moment or what would have followed. For, just then, Teacher's wife seemed to have realised that her action had created a situation which was more serious than she had expected. Her only desire was to escape from it. In reply to the Inspector's question, she said, "No, mahaswami."

"Is she a pupil?" the Inspector asked.

"Mahaswami," said Teacher.

"Yes," his wife replied.

The Inspector looked at Teacher. "You certainly have caught hold of a mature one, haven't you?"

"Mahaswami."

"What class are you in?" the Inspector asked her.

There was anger on her face. She walked to the door muttering, "A mature one, is it? Who is he then, a tender lemon?"

Watching her leave the room, the Inspector turned to our teacher. "What's this, ayya? She walked away without saying anything. What class is she in?"

"Mahaswami."

The Inspector was annoyed. "What's the matter with you? All you have done is repeated mahaswami, mahaswami."

"Mahaswami," Teacher said, once again.

"Was she annoyed?"

"May be, mahaswami."

"Yes. It was not right for me to call her a mature one," the Inspector said. Then, he added, "Shall we get on with the inspection?"

"You must be exhausted after your journey, mahaswami. Why don't we have the inspection tomorrow?"

"All right. Let's have a song from someone who sings well, then."

The best singer in the class was Lakshmi. Teacher turned to her and said, "Come on, Lakshmi. Let's have you sing the one on King George."

Lakshmi stood up. The kitten was still on her lap. The Inspector Went up to her in order to hear her clearly. As Lakshmi started to sing, the kitten, which had been sitting comfortably in the folds of her dress, woke up, and started to fidget. It wanted to get out.

The Inspector's eyes fell on the moving folds of her dress. He pointed to it and asked, "What's that, there?"

Lakshmi was in two minds. She did not know what to say. She looked at me. "Your baby?" asked the Inspector, who could have had a grandchild as old as Lakshmi. At the same time, he put his hand out to find out what it was. The kitten was angry, since it could not get out. Soon it would have scratched Lakshmi's stomach. When the Inspector's hand reached it, it attacked!

I have already told you about Garudamari's paws, and how they could scratch. Now, the Inspector too found out. Pulling his hand back as fast as he could, he shouted, "What kind of a school is this? That girl walks out in anger, this one brings a kitten with her. What is going on?"

There was helplessness in the teachers's reply. "Mahaswami, only God knows what I go through. As the girls grow older, they tend to lose their temper faster. You can't tell them to study. They run away from the school. The little girls want their kittens. If we ask them not to bring the kittens here, they stay away too. If I have stayed on as a teacher, it is mainly because I do not want to be disloyal to the hand, like yours, that feeds me. You saw it yourself. My rib-cage has gone dry trying to teach in this school."

"Tell me, what's your salary?"

"Ten rupees for a month's hard work, mahaswan1i."

"Don't worry. I'll write today itself and recommend that your salary should be increased to twelve rupees a month."

That was the end of the school for the day.

Three days ago Teacher visited us. When I had gone to say goodbye to him before leaving the place after my marriage, he had said, "I had told you that you would be blessed with a good husband. And things have turned out that way. I shall visit you one day. Think of us sometimes."

And he had come to visit. He wanted me to talk to my husband about getting him a promotion. My husband said he would help. When I told him this story of our teacher, he laughed heartily. Thanks to my husband, Teacher was promoted and was entitled to a higher salary. His second visit was to thank us.

He said to me, "She is not there now, Sitamma, to benefit from your help." I did not have to ask him who "she" was. A man may have many a "she" in his life these days, but not then.

"What happened, Teacher?" I asked.

"Ammayya, she died leaving behind a girl child," he said. "I have to look after my daughter, now." There were tears in his eyes as he added, "She had a hard time throughout. If she were here today, I would have bought her a new saree. She would have been thrilled. I wasn't fortunate enough to do such a thing."

I was too moved to say anything. After a pause, he continued, "Her love for me was boundless, Sitamma. She held my feet that day and said, It's time for me to go. Don't hold any anger against me. I put you to trouble many times. I told her, You gave me no trouble but I didn't give you any happiness. She said, You don't know this. I was happy but I didn't realise it either. Now that the time has come for us to part, I know it. Her love was the life-giving kind, Sitamma. She was utterly guileless. I know her speech was rather rough. But she had a heart which was like butter. Let me give you an example of it. Do you remember the day when the Inspector came? I went home and told her that the Inspector had decided to recommend me for a promotion. She said, May be it is because he thought I was a pupil and realised how difficult it must be to teach someone like me. You better tell him the truth. I told her that the Inspector was probably afraid that someone would find out that he had called her a mature one. She said, He has no sense. Is that the way to talk in a girls' school? It doesn't matter to us what sort of a man he is. Tell him the reason for my coming to school, that I am not a pupil.

"Sitamma, believe me or not, I told the Inspector the truth. At first, he was angry. But then he laughed loudly and said, I recommended a salary of twelve rupees a month because I thought she was a pupil. Had I known that she was your wife, I would have raised it to fifteen. So that was your wife. Ayyo! ... Poor fellow, what did he know?"

Teacher was silent for a while, thinking ...

Is there anyone who knows everything about another's life?

Venkatashami's Love Affair

During the holidays this time, I went to Ramaswamy's village. One evening, on our way back from the new orchard he was getting planted, we stopped to sit under a tree. It was a lovely spot. We could see a tank-bund in the distance. There was an open paddy field below it. To its right was a mango grove and to its left, the fields belonging to the villagers.

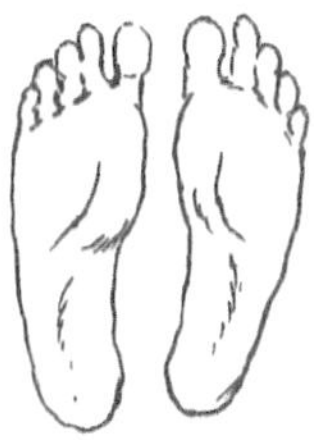

The water from the tank flowed through the field and into a narrow canal beside the place where we were sitting. We could see a square green plot at the edge of the fields in front of us. The cattle had already gone home and there was no one around. The sun's rays fell on the land, the fields and the grove, making their colours glow. A cool breeze was blowing. It was as if one could stretch out one's hand and grab the evening peace that was coming down from the sky. I, who had grown up in the city, learnt a little about the happiness of life in a village that evening. I told Ramaswamy that it was a beautiful place.

"Yes," he said. "It is the loveliest spot in the village. That is why my father planted this tree here and I put up the stone bench under it."

"And someone else who thought like you, planted that grove. The plot, with a tree at each comer and one in the centre, is a panchavati," I said.

"You're right. Venkatashami, our barber's son, lies buried there.

The field belongs to his father. Before he died, the boy had asked to be buried at this spot. The father carried out his son's last wish. He planted the trees. That neem tree in the centre stands at the head of the grave. It is a love story."

"A love story? "Why don't you tell it to me?"

Ramaswamy began ...

Venkatashami was about ten years older than me. He left our school when I was in the first standard. His father, Narasappa, was very keen that his son should learn to read and write. The boy did go to school for a short while, but had enough of it by the time he was on his second reader. His heart was not in his studies even when he attended his classes. All he wanted was to sling a small bag on his shoulder and carry on his father's profession. And he had a very deft hand. The teachers in the school used to wait for an auspicious day before they sent for Narasa. But when Venkatashami grew up, they would send for him and ask for a shave whenever they felt like it. The father let his son do what he wanted, confident that the boy would earn his living somehow.

Around that time, a troupe of acrobats visited our village. Our Ramegowda was known to be a very generous man, and the leader of the group was heard to say that they were here just for that reason. The villagers were happy that someone else was paying, while they enjoyed the show. We were youngsters at that time and in our excitement we thought that heaven had descended on earth. The show was to be held the next day. It was our luck that our teacher went down with temperature and school was closed for the day. The acrobats' visit turned out to be a festive occasion for us. It commanded the same respect as the Deputy Commissioner's. The whole village turned out at the performance.

I will not say anything about how good the show was. To us, everything was wonderful, from the series of cartwheels by the young Dombara boys, to the revolutions on top of a small bamboo pole by their leader. Even the grown-ups could not help but appreciate it. But what amazed everyone was the way the Dombara girl did her act. I have seen many bamboo poles since then, but they do not look as big as the one I saw that day. If a person fell off such a pole, he was not likely to Survive.

When I saw the girl go up the tall pole that day, I thought she must have touched the sky. She looked like a squirrel running up a Coconut tree as she climbed up. She was wearing a saree, tightly wrapped around her body, a close-fitting blouse and had a strong band tied around her waist. She quickly reached the top, balanced herself on the head of the pole and performed some feats, now lying on her back and now on her belly. And then came the spin. Resting the weight of her body on one hand, she started to go round and round slowly. Then as her speed increased, she stretched out her limbs. At first, we could tell her hands from her legs. But when she went round faster and faster, she looked like a rapidly spinning wheel.

In the beginning, the spectators whispered appreciatively to each other, "See how well she does this!" Then, they said, "Look! She has let go of her hand!" But when she started gyrating at top speed, they held their breaths in fear and wished in their heart of hearts that she would come down unharmed. Her brother stood on one side, banging on a small drum, while her father sat on the other side beating a big one. Her mother sat next to him, intently watching her daughter. When the spinning had gone on for some time, the Gowda told the leader of the Dombaras that it was enough, and suggested that the performance could end. The man said, "It is almost over, swami." The girl had gradually stopped spinning. She then stood on the end of the bamboo, balancing on her left foot, did a namaskara to the crowd and came sliding down the supporting rope on the side. She covered herself with a cloth and sat down beside her mother.

I was a young boy at that time, but even I had wanted to go on looking at her in that dress. What can one say about how the older people felt? There were grown-up boys in our teacher's household and the Gowda's. They too came to our school. For the next three days, their talk was only about the girl. It must have been the same with the adults. But the traditionalists among them were not in a position to indulge in such talk. We had a couple of rasikas in the village. I think they too were silent out of a fear of the others. Since there were no gossip-mongers, these people behaved sensibly, I suppose.

The acrobats stayed for a day more, and after they received their gifts from the Gowda, left for the neighbouring village. That was the end of the affair as far as the boys were concerned. But from the point of view of the village, a problem was left behind.

On the day the Dombaras left our village, Venkatashami and some others accompanied them. They returned after a short while, but Venkatashami said he would come back later. He did not come home that day. The following day, a man from the next village brought the news that Venkatashami was with the Dombaras and had told somebody, half jokingly, that he was going to marry the girl. The news reached our village. There was lamenting in Venkatashami's family. The villagers were a little concerned.

Venkatashami's mother, Muniyamma, called her husband and asked him, "Shouldn't you go and bring the boy home?" It seemed he had not heard what she said. She became a little more insistent and reminded him of his duty as the boy's father. Even then, Narasappa did not budge. So Muniyamma scolded, "What kind of a man are you? How can you stand and watch your son go the wrong way?"

Only the previous year, the matter of Venkatashami's marriage had come up but Muniyamma had brushed it aside saying, "Not so soon." Narasa reminded her of this and taunted her, "When I told you the boy has come of age, let us bring a daughter-in-law, you said No, because you were afraid to lose your position as the mistress of the household. Now suffer for that!"

"All right, all right, enough of this master and mistress business. That boy might tie the knot with the Dombara girl. Go and bring him back before that," she retorted.

"Ai, mistress, hold your tongue," he said. "That boy of yours wasn't born to a Dombara for him to go and marry one. She must have just smiled at him and he must have stood there, gaping. Why make so much noise for that? Wait for a couple of days, he is sure to come back," he said and ended the discussion. Unable to think of anything else, Muniyamma went and complained to the Gowda.

The Gowda was sitting in the chavadi with some of the elders of the village when Muniyamma's ranting interrupted their conversation.

The Gowda could not ignore the matter as Narasa had done. He was worried about the affair bringing a bad name to the village. An acrobat girl picking up the son of the village barber was like a hunter's hound being carried away by a fox. It would be a blow to his prestige as the headman of the village. He sent for the gardener Mariga, and told him, "Marigya, go and bring Venkatashami and the leader of the acrobats here." Muniyamma went home, relieved. The Gowda would somehow save the boy.

There was no need for Mariga to go and fetch Venkatashami. The boy himself came home just as Narasa had sat down to his meal.

"Ai Shamiga, why didn't you come home yesterday evening?" Muniyamma asked her son. Not giving him a chance to speak, Narasa cut in, "He had some work in the neighbouring village, so he stayed back. Why this cross-examination?"

Venkatashami had a wash and sat down beside his father. His mother was impatient to bring up the matter of the girl and settle it once for all, but had a suspicion that her husband would not allow any discussion. She served food to her son but her mind was elsewhere. Halfway through the meal, Venkatashami turned to his father and said, "There is something I want to ask you, Appaji."

"What is it?"

"The other day when I went to the big house to give the young master a shave, he praised me and told me I had a very fine hand. There was no one like me even in Bangalore, and if I worked there, I could earn thirty rupees a month, he said. I have decided to go to Bangalore, Appaji."

"Ai Shamlga, it's enough if you ask your father, is it? There's no need to tell your mother?" complained Muniyamma.

"Will I ever go away without asking you, Amma? I brought it up now because both of you are here."

"You can go. I have no objection," said his father.

"I'm thinking of leaving tomorrow or the day after."

"Let's see. We must ask our shanbogh and our Gowda. It's a matter of your leaving the place. They should say Yes, shouldn't they?"

"You are prepared to send him to Bangalore if they agree? We have only one son. What do you want to do after sending our only child to Bangalore? Have a jolly time with me?" Muniyamma said.

"What's this, mistress of the house, you are opening your mouth too much? Is it because your son has grown up? You had better keep quiet." Muniyamma became silent, mumbling something under her breath.

To tell the truth, Venkatashami's father was filled with fear. He suspected that this trip to Bangalore had something to do with the Dombara girl. He would not have minded if the boy had had a brief affair with her. He would have to hang his head in front of the people, but he could have explained it saying that the boy was foolish and immature. But now, his very existence in the village seemed to be threatened. The boy would leave for Bangalore and a new barber would be appointed. He would lose his inamati, the land his family had been given, for the duties they had performed for the community. Not that he got much out of the land. But the prestige and the importance of being a functionary of the village was what really mattered. What was the way out? If the boy had brought up the matter of the girl, he could have told him that these things are not done. But the boy had denied him the chance to utter his words of advice. As a father, he was in no position to bring up such matters with his grown-up son. Not knowing what to do, Narasa finished his lunch and went to see the Gowda.

Muniyamma was waiting for just this moment. Barely had he left, when she said, "Ela Shamiga, the people of the village are saying all sorts of things. Should you give them reason for such gossip, annaji?"

"What are they saying, Aroma?"

"That you are besotted with a Dombara girl, and that you are always in her company."

"It's true, Aroma."

"It isn't right, you should know that."

"Right or not, I can't live without her, Aroma."

"How can you say such a thing? Shouldn't you bother about your parents' prestige and about what others of our caste will say?"

"That's why this decision to go to Bangalore."

"Is she also going with you?"

"She may. We cannot set up a home here anyway. Let me see if we can do it in Bangalore."

"Forgetting your own parents ..."

"Why should I forget you, Aroma? I'll send you money."

"Will I have to say I have a Dombara for a daughter-in-law, then?"

"That girl is like pure gold, Aroma."

"Yes, yes, annaji. She's pure gold in your eyes, in the eyes of all those who see her ..." Muniyamma sat down and wept.

Venkatashami was very serious when he said all those things. But seeing no end to the discussion, he walked out into the street. If Muniyamma had come out, she would have realised that he was heading for the village where the group of acrobats had camped.

When Narasa reached the Gowda's place, the leader of the Dombaras was seated there. "Mahaswami, you are the head of this village. What will happen to us if you don't look into the matter and set it right? We eat crows, they eat chicken. Now this boy comes and asks for my daughter's hand in marriage. How can we hope to make our living if he runs away with the girl? I have grown old, my wife is in no condition to climb the pole. The other children are small. If we break the pole and use it for firewood, what show can we put up?"

Narasa had arrived just as the Gowda was asking the man, "Can't you tell your girl not to go with him?"

The Gowda turned to him and said, "You have come about your son, I suppose?" Narasa did not say anything.

The girl's father replied, "We did speak to her, mahaswami. She too isn't happy to go away from her parents. But her heart seems to flutter when she sees the youth. She has been crying. 1 somehow managed to drive him out of our camp. Can't think of a show for the next few days. Suppose she slips and falls because her mind is somewhere else? You are a big dhani. We came here hoping to prosper by your generosity. Now things have turned out this way."

Venkatashami's father heard these words and was reassured. He told the Gowda, "I came here to say the same thing. Both he and I are agreed on saying No. So there should not be a problem. A few elders should express their disapproval of the whole thing, that's all."

After further discussion, it was decided that the Dombaras should go far away from the village and a close watch should be kept on Venkatashami. The two men left for their respective homes.

The acrobat troupe went away. But was there any place, so far, that Venkatashami could not hope to reach it? Actually, it wasn't all that far. To those of us who live on the plains, anything beyond the fourth village is far away. Our villages are so close that one can easily reach out and touch the neighbouring village. A young man can travel this distance ten times in a day, if he wants to.

Venkatashami did not give up visiting the girl. His mother kept scolding and shouting but his father showed his anger by maintaining a sullen silence. Venkatashami did not care.

Every Sunday some of us boys used to roam in the woods beyond the tank and look for fruit – karehannu, mirupehannu and budumekai. One Sunday, we saw Venkatashami there with the girl. He had a bow in his hand and he was shooting crows for her. Some of the big boys in our gang saw them and what he was doing. They started laughing. The girl covered her face with her pallu, but Venkatashami did not seem to be embarrassed at all. I did not understand why my companions were laughing. Soon word got around in the village that the barber's boy had started shooting crows to win the heart of a girl. Even now we have a proverb in our place, Wanting to befriend the Dombaras, a barber even ate a dog.*

It seems it was either that day or the day after, that Mariappa from the Gowda's household was going along this road. He thought he saw two figures standing on the grass. Mariappa was not one to be frightened of anything other than ghosts. Wanting to make sure it was not a pair of spirits, he asked, "Who is it?"

"It's me, Marianna," the boy replied, "What are you doing here at this hour?"

"One of our cows is missing, I came looking for it. aha, it's Venkatashami, is it? All right." As he turned to go, he said, "Anyway, you seem to have found one."

Venkatashami had nothing to say in reply to Mariappa's joke.

A few days later, when everyone had gone to sleep, Venkatashami came home and knocked on the door. His mother did not open it. When the boy knocked again, his father said, "Why don't you open the door? Shall I?" She replied, "Go and lie down quietly. There's no need to open it for that stupid fool. This is not a prostitute's house for the door to open whenever he comes." Venkatashami heard his mother's words. He knew she had deliberately not let him in. He went away.

For a few days no one knew where Venkatashami had gone. Enquiries revealed that he had run away with the Dombara girl. The leader of the troupe came to the Gowda to express his grief and went back to the camp. There was nothing that anyone could do. Four days later, a Gowda from a village some five miles away,

* The proverb in Kannada that Masti gives here reads: *Dombara jote dosti madi nayinda nayi tinda.* Half its appeal is in the alliteration between pairs of words and the juxtaposition of nayi (dog) and nayinda (barber).

was passing this way, and he brought Venkatashami and left him at his parents' house. The boy was burning with fever. It seems the girl was with him when he became ill. She had been taken home by her father and Venkatashami had been brought back, seriously ill.

The boy did not recover from that illness. He was a handsome boy with an open face. Dark, yes, but attractive. The black of his skin, that of his eyes, and of his moustache were of three different shades. When he smiled, it was like a flash of lightning among the clouds. His body was so well-built, no hammer could break it. The fever that had caught hold of him seemed unwilling to let go of such a fine physique. They call the fever by the name typhoid now and can diagnose it in no time. But those days, nobody was aware of such things. All they knew was that something was wrong with the tongue. He was given the traditional medicines and kept on a local diet. A fortnight later Venkatashami passed away. His delirious mind rambled and his talk was all about his meetings with the girl. Whenever he was conscious, he kept asking them to call her. It would have been all right if he had been married to her. His request would have been treated with understanding and sympathy, and she would have been sent for. But does one bring the girl who had led him astray, to his bedside in these circumstances?

In the end, Venkatashami did not see her again. He probably knew he was dying. He said to his father, "Appa, I am asking you for something. Will you do it?"

"Why, what is the matter, anna?"

"Nothing, Appa. My act is over. You must make a place for me on the grassy patch near our field."

Someone standing by the bedside said, "What is this? Fine talk, indeed!"

"I don't care whether it's fine or not. If I don't tell them, they will bury me just anywhere. I want to be buried there, nowhere else," Venkatashami insisted.

"Why should you bother about it? You will be gone anyway," the man said.

"I don't have strength to talk any more. Promise me, Appa ..." the boy pleaded.

"Very well, annaji."

Venkatashami paused for a minute, then said, "We spent three nights there." I think those were his last words.

He was buried at this spot according to his wishes. These trees were planted by his parents. When I was young, I remember, I used to be quite scared to pass this way ...

That was the end of my friend's story. I wanted to know what happened to the girl. Ramaswamy did not know. "Didn't you feel like finding out?" I asked. "If it were now, perhaps I would have been curious. Or I would have found out at least for the sake of a storyteller like you. We weren't bothered about all those things at that time," he replied.

Just then, an old villager came to where we were sitting. "What brings you here, swami?" he asked Ramaswamy.

"This gentleman is my friend. I told him Venkatashami's story," he said.

"Hn," the old man replied. "But see what happened? Because of him, an outsider had to step into our barber's shoes and take away the income."

"Poor fellow. He died young. If he had lived, there was so much happiness life could have given him," I said, adding, "How does it matter, who does the job of a barber?"

"All that is Bangalore talk, swami," the old man retorted. "We villagers don't think like that. An outsider should not spread his cloth to collect what is a hereditary entitlement. We cannot even talk to him as we can to our own barber, swami."

My mind was caught in a whirl with Venkatashami's tale,

Ramaswamy's indifference and the old man's fierce pride and attachment to his village.

All three of us walked away.

I have told you what I learnt from Ramaswamy. I do not know whether you consider it a story or not. Thinking of Venkatashami and the girl, I have experienced some pleasure and much pain. I do not know what your feelings are at the end of this narration. I only hope that you have not been bored. Never mind what you felt. Think of the love between the boy and the girl, of their walking together on this road, near the tank, by the forest and on the grass beside the field. And of the end of their love with the boy's death. I am sure you will be moved by the fate of the barber's boy and the girl he lost.

Jogyora Anjappa's Chicken

Jogyora Anjappa is the oldest among the old people of our village. Whenever he gets a chance, he starts talking about things that had happened when he was a mere boy. There is no one alive now who could have seen the events he talks about. He claims he was a boy at the time of the Sepoy Mutiny. When we ask him his age, he says he must be about a hundred

years old. He has been a hundred for the last ten years. The main thing is that because of his age, Anjappa has acquired the authority to advise everyone, whatever the matter or the occasion. While the people may have some doubts about his assumed authority, he has absolutely none. When Anjappa advised you to do this or do that, and you did not follow his advice immediately, he would say, "What's this, fellow? My beard had become grey even when your father was a little child, and you take my words so lightly?" As a result of the vast experience he has had, the advice he gives is generally sound. In years he was a veritable Jambavanta, and in the sharpness of his mind, a Hanumantha.

Three days ago, Anjappa had gone to see Rangappa. Just a few days earlier, Rangappa had received the order appointing him Bench Magistrate of our taluka. Everyone in our village was delighted that our shanbogh now had the authority to put someone behind bars. It was a symbol of great power and prestige to be able to do that, they thought. If nothing else, a man holding the office of bench magistrate was the equal of a subedar. Earlier, only someone the rank of a subedar or higher, had this authority. They believed that the government had now taken it away even from a subedar. If you look at it like that, the man to whom this position is given, holds a rank higher than a subedar's, even if it is so, only by as much as the weight of a gulagunji seed! And so, the seniormost elder of the village had come to have a chat with the shanbogh, and to give him some timely advice.

"Come, Anjappa. Sit down," Rangappa said to him.

"So, you have been made the magistrate. Very happy to hear that."

"Happy all right, Anjappa. But, what's there in it? Just some work without any wages. No money, nothing."

"No money? Why not?"

"One does the bench magistrate's work for the prestige. The government doesn't pay a salary for it."

"Why should you say that there's no money just because there's no salary? Didn't salaried officers think of their salary as small change? If their salary was one, their income was ten."

"Those days are gone, Anjappa. You can't take bribes and all that now."

"Those who want to will, those who don't want to, will not. But never mind. Tell me, if you ever get angry, do you now have the authority to summon the subedar and fine him?"

"May be if you were the magistrate, you could have done it. I'm only a shanbogh. If I fine the subedar, he will dismiss me saying that I haven't submitted the accounts."

Anjappa thought that there was a point in what Rangappa said. He took out his sanchi, the cloth bag with his betel leaves and nuts, and started sorting them out. Most of the leaves and the nuts in it were old, just like him. Though he bought fresh betel leaves now and then, he would still chew the dried up ones first, saying, "Ayyo, these leaves are getting spoilt." He did not like to throw them away. By the time he finished the old ones, the fresh ones he had bought would have begun to wilt! The betel nuts in his sanchi too, were famous.

It is only the ignorant who think that betel nuts are to be chewed and swallowed along with the leaves. The real purpose of the nut is to make the mouth water, not become water itself. It should stay in the mouth for a while, get soaked in the saliva, and then be pulverised along with the leaf. If it gets soft as soon as it is popped into the mouth, imagine the quantity of nuts that will be required by someone who is used to chewing leaves all the time! Anjappa took out a withered leaf and a small nut and put them into his mouth. Then taking a small piece of chunam from the tin, he said, "Never mind all that. I have come here to tell you something."

"What is it, Anjappa? You are a man with rich experience. There must be a hundred things that people like me must learn from you."

"That's why I am here. Now you have become a magistrate. When people are brought before you, you must be able to clearly say this man is honest, this one is a thief, and then award punishment. You shouldn't go only by what the police or the lawyers say. I just came to tell you that."

"That's all right, Anjappa. But how will I know whether a man is honest or a thief, unless I listen to what others say about him? There's no other way a magistrate can find out."

"Once a man calls himself a magistrate, he should try to get at the truth. He should address himself to the man brought before him."

"Anjappa, don't get angry if I ask you something."

"Go ahead and ask. Why should I get angry?"

"Tell me, was there a charge against you in the court of a magistrate?"

"You are asking me! That's what I came here to tell you about. They made a complaint that I had stolen a chicken. I said I had not. They insisted I had. Finally, the charge was upheld. If you pay a fine of twenty rupees, we will let you go. Otherwise, a term in jail, they said. I paid the fine and walked out with dignity."

"How did they decide that you had stolen the chicken? Did they find it with you?"

"Yes, Rangappa, they did. It's because that wretched bird was found on me, that I got caught."

"It means that you had stolen it, doesn't it?"

"No, and that's what I'm trying to tell you. True, the bird was in my possession. But I hadn't stolen it."

"Go on, then. Tell us what really happened ..."

And Anjappa told him the story.

This must have taken place some forty years or more ago, when Anjappa was already a middle-aged man. In those days, his profession took him from Village to village. The profession of a jogi meant dressing up in a resplendent costume, carrying a cloth jholi on the left shoulder and a kindari on the right, and wandering around singing songs that had come down from one's grandfather's time, seeking alms. In the days of Anjappa's ancestors, jogis did not till the land. They lived only on what they received from the people. But in these bad times, they too have taken to farming. Anjappa described this as being similar to a brahmin keeping a footwear shop in the market. To you and me, asking for alms might seem contemptible, but not to Anjappa.

"It's nota joke, becoming a jogi," he would say. "Wandering around for twenty years, with father or uncle, carrying the kindari, singing songs along with them, learning the job, it is not easy. Any boy can stand behind the plough, twist the tail of the bullock and goad it, saying choh! chon! To learn a song, don't you need a voice? Intelligence? By just saying oon ... oon ... does it become a song? You need a fine tongue to master the words. Not everyone can say Lakshmi properly. Ksmi, Ksmi, they say, as if they are about to sneeze. Nor is it easy to shape your mouth to pronounce Draupadadevi. By the time I could become a professional jogi, I was twenty-five years old. Then, my father said, Not bad, not bad at all. Now you can stand on your own feet. In other words, becoming a proper jogi is as difficult as getting a BA degree these days."

I think Anjappa used to cover some sixty or seventy villages on his rounds. A jogi does not leave his house like any ordinary beggar. Just as an actor playing the role of a king on the stage paints his cheeks, his lips, his moustache, a jogi who goes round singing must also dress in the traditional manner before he sets out.

A jogi is not a Shaiva or a Vaishnava. Nor does he worship the minor deities. But he has not given up any of them, either. That is why one can see all three – vibhuti, kumkuma and turmeric – on his forehead. He uses collyrium for his eyes, to prevent his normally fierce stare from harming the people. Unless he does this, his penetrating gaze is sure to hurt them, especially when he sings songs about Bheema and Hanumantha, and send them into a swoon.

Just as his face was painted in a special way, his robes too had to be distinct, and his turban made of rags of at least three colours. Anjappa had been handsome in his youth. So it was not surprising that as he walked along in his colourful dress, singing songs, all the women and children of the village gathered around him. They made him sit in front of the big Gowda's house, and listened to him. He would often say, "I have sung so many songs and given pleasure to so many people." In those days, forty years ago, his jogi's profession was at its peak and he was very popular with most people.

One of the places Anjappa used to visit on his rounds was Kalapura. That is not the real name of the place I have in mind. If, by any chance, there is a place by that name, I would like you to understand that I am not referring to it. Kalapura is a name I have made up. It was a reasonably big place, so Anjappa would stay there for a couple of days on his visits. I have already said Anjappa was handsome, haven't I? We must keep that detail in mind. So, when he went into the village with his make-up and his costume, it was only natural that a number of women were charmed by him – as natural as women's admiration for a handsome stage actor. Anjappa did not mind sitting and chatting with women who were no longer very young because there was nobody to scold them for it. But if they were younger, Anjappa would hesitate, for if the men of the house saw him, they would say, "What's this, jogi? Instead of taking your bhiksha and going away, you are fooling around with our women? Get out." And the outsiders would say, with a smile, "Not bad, jogyappa!" Both these comments are not good for a man who lives on alms.

Once, when Anjappa visited Kalapura, the Gowda's wife asked him to sing a song for her. She was the Gowda's third wife. When he had finished she offered him betel leaves and nuts. He was still sitting there, talking to her, when her husband came and shouted at him. Anjappa was not the type to answer back. But the Gowda used some had words and that infuriated Anjappa.

"You have said some very offensive things to me, Gowda-re. If you are a man with any self-respect, talk to your wife. Don't abuse me."

The Gowda was enraged. "Watch it, jogi, or one day I'll kill you," he shouted. Anjappa said a few things himself in reply, picked up his bag and walked away.

Anjappa went to Kalapura a couple of times after this incident, but nothing unusual happened.

On his third visit there, he was sitting and singing on the jagali of a house in one of the localities. A girl from the neighbouring house was standing by her door, listening to him. When he finished and was about to leave, she called him and gave him bhiksha. Anjappa went there again the following day. The girl asked him to sit outside her house and sing. For a house in the village, it was quite big. Anjappa enquired who the house belonged to and whose daughter the girl was. I do not remember the name now. It was a well-to-do family. The girl's husband was known to have taken to evil ways. The girl also was not all that good, it seems.

Anjappa did not know about it then. There were three of them in the family – the girl, her husband and her mother-in-law. They had a poultry and did business in chickens. When Anjappa went to Kalapura again, he went to the girl's house. She was good-looking. Anjappa had no evil motive behind his visit, but he enjoyed singing to her because she made her pleasure and admiration for him so obvious. After he finished singing in that neighbourhood and all the people had left, he went to her house to sit at her door and chew his betel leaves.

After a while, the girl came out and said, "Jogyappa, before you leave the village, please come this way."

"Why, amma? I'm about to go now. What do you want me to do?" Anjappa asked.

"Your songs have made me very happy. I have often thought of giving you something to show my appreciation. You must take it and go away immediately. If my mother-in-law finds out she will scream at me:"

Anjappa was a little hesitant about taking the gift. But he did not want to refuse it either. Before he could say anything, the girl ran inside and called him in. As soon as he went in, she put a chicken into his bag and almost published him out saying, "Go, go!" Anjappa went off without thinking too much about what he was doing, though his heart was pounding at the thought of what might happen if someone were to catch him. "Be careful, jogyappa, and don't ever tell anyone that I gave you the chicken," the girl cried out from inside. Anjappa walked off without saying anything. There was a well half a mile away from the village. He stopped only when he reached it, and sat down in the shade of a tree to have his betel leaf and think about the events of the day.

This was the first time that such a thing had happened to Anjappa and he did not want it to happen again. A chicken is an expensive item. Why should anyone give a chicken to a jogi for nothing? There are two ways of giving bhiksha. One is to do it openly. There is nothing underhand about it. The other is to give it secretly, and deceit is part of this. Anjappa had liked the girl. Such a good girl! So pretty too. Like a ripe lemon, he thought. How could a husband go astray with a girl like that for a wife? That is life! The rich ones are wastrels, the poor ones have to become thieves.

As he sat there thinking about all this, Anjappa had forgotten that it was not safe for him to remain in that place. A little while later, a man coming from the village stopped near him.

"How are you, jogyappa? Resting?" he asked.

"Yes," Anjappa replied.

"So, your jholi is full?"

"The same as usual."

"Ragi, is it ?" said the man, peering into the bag. "What's this?" he exclaimed. "A chicken!"

A tremorran through Anjappa's body. "Someone gave it to me," he explained. Before any more questions were asked, about who gave it, he picked up his jholi and got ready to leave. Just then, he noticed an elderly woman walking quickly towards him. She was accompanied by a man. A few paces behind them was the girl who had gifted him the chicken. Anjappa's knees turned to water. He could not take a step forward. He realised that he was in great trouble. As he waited for the man and woman to come closer, he saw the girl gesturing to him, asking him not to tell them the truth about the chicken. The old lady came up to Anjappa, then asked the man with her, "Is this the jogyappa?" "Yes," said the man. He was the talari, the watchman of the village.

"Jogyappa, have you seen one of our chickens?" the woman asked.

"Some wretched bird has got into my bag without my knowledge. This man here showed it to me," Anjappa replied.

"Didn't you say that it was given to you?" the man asked.

"Ayyol It's so difficult for a jogi to get even a handful of rice these days, who will give him a chicken?" Anjappa told him.

The talari emptied the bag. The chicken was there, lying half dead.

"Not bad! We allow him near the house because he sings songs. Then he starts to steal our chickens" the old woman observed. "Come to the village. Let's speak to the Gowda. Fine jogi you are," she scolded.

"Amma, I didn't steal the chicken. If it is yours, take it. Just leave me alone," Anjappa said.

"Listen to him talk ... as if he is some virtuous man! If you didn't steal it, how is the chicken with you?" she wanted to know. Turning to the girl, she asked her, "Isn't this ours?"

The girl was evasive in her reply. "May be it is ours. May be it isn't. I can't say. The jogi might have bought it somewhere."

The talari intervened at that stage. "There's no point talking about it here. Come, let's go to the Gowda and tell him everything. He will decide who's right."

Anjappa could see no way out of this. The Gowda was still angry with him. It was his rotten luck, he told himself, as he walked back to the village with his bag of alms.

There is no point narrating all that happened there.

All those who had lost their chickens before this, and even those who hadn't, remembered having missed them after Anjappa had visited their locality. The Gowda arrived. "Ai, jogi, you thought you were a singer, did you? Wait till you are sent to the lock-up. That's when you will be really singing." The police station was not far away.

They sent the accused there with a report and the incriminating evidence. Statements were taken from the people concerned, and Anjappa came out on bail, after promising to present himself before the court on the day of the trial.

The trial was held. What was the crime to investigate, anyway? The old woman had lost a chicken. It was found in Anjappa's possession. Three witnesses were present when she identified the bird as hers. The magistrate asked Anjappa whether he had anything to say.

"Mahaswami, while I was singing, the chicken might have got into the bag thinking it was warm inside. I was not aware of it and I took it along with me," Anjappa said.

"What nonsense is this? Who has heard of a chicken getting into a bag? Tell the truth," the magistrate ordered.

"It is the truth, mahaswami. I'm prepared to swear in the name of any god you want me to. I didn't steal the chicken."

"Let us suppose you didn't steal it. The chicken didn't walk into your bag, Tell me, did someone give it to you?"

Anjappa could have said that the girl gave it to him. The words were on the tip of his tongue. But he remembered that she had made him promise not to say anything to anyone, and how she had signalled to him to keep quiet. Something had made her give him the chicken and he did not want to betray her. So he held back his words. Again the magistrate asked him for an answer.

"What can I say, mahaswami? You are the ultimate authority in all matters of dharma. Only God can tell you what the truth is. I didn't steal the chicken."

The magistrate chargesheeted him and asked him whether he had any witnesses to support his statement.

"Ayyo, mahaswami, God is my only witness," Anjappa told him. The magistrate was impressed with his speech. "Even if he is a thief, see how well he speaks," he said and sentenced him to a fine of twenty rupees or imprisonment for fifteen days. Anjappa paid the fine and went back to his village, with a sad face.

All this happened, as I told you, some forty years ago.

When he came to the end of this story, Anjappa said, "It's not enough to become a magistrate. It is God's work to punish the guilty and protect the honest. If that work has to be done by a man, he must act like God. He must always be careful not to make a mistake. Otherwise, he will be unjust, like the magistrate who wanted to put handcuffs on me."

"That is right, Anjappa," I said. "But how do you expect a magistrate to know the truth unless you tell him what really happened?"

"Why do we need intelligent people like you to dispense justice, then, if all that you do is base your decisions on what people say? It's the magistrate's job to find out the truth."

"You paid the fine to save the girl's honour. You did a good thing, Anjappa."

"Ayyo! What do you know about it? It seems that girl was on intimate terms with a man and had given him the chickens two or three times before this. When her mother-in-law had asked her about the missing birds, she had said that someone must have stolen them. The old lady didn't believe her. So the girl waited for an occasion when she could point out to someone who had a chicken in his possession. That would help her to cover up her cheating on earlier occasions, wouldn't it? That's why she did all this. I came to know about it much later."

"What? You are saying that she first gave you the chicken and then told her mother-in-law?"

"Hn, that's exactly what happened. The old lady came in. She found the chicken missing. She asked the girl, who said she didn't know anything about it. The mother-in-law wanted to know whether anyone had passed that way. At first, she said she didn't know, then added that the jogi had come. The neighbour confirmed it saying that he had seen the jogi walking away quickly from there. Well, everything fell into place and I was caught."

"Didn't you go and ask the girl whether it was right for her to do such a thing?" Rangappa asked.

"Rangappa, you are all still young. I'm an old man. Why do you want to know what happened in my youth? Yes. I did go and ask her ... I did everything ..."

We did net ask for any more details.

Finally, Rangappa said, "If ever you stand accused in my presence, I'll find out the truth and let you off, believe me."

"Now I will not be judged by any man. The only magistrate for me will be Venkataramanaswamy of Tirupati. I will stand before him and admit I made a mistake. I will fall at his feet. He will take care of me."

We kept quiet. Anjappa sat there for some more time. Then he said to Rangappa, "Won't you give me some betelnuts and leaves, now that you are a magistrate?"

Rangappa sent a boy to fetch some. Anjappa took them.

As he left, he told us, "Remember what I have told you."

The Pandit's Will

Vishalaksha Pandit became the chief minister soon after Chikkadevaraja Wodeyar came to the throne. The Raja had known the Pandit since his boyhood, when he had lived with his father in Hangala. At that time, the Pandit, a caste brahmin but of the Jain faith, lived in Chamarajanagar, on the earnings from his ancestral property and his profession as an astrologer.

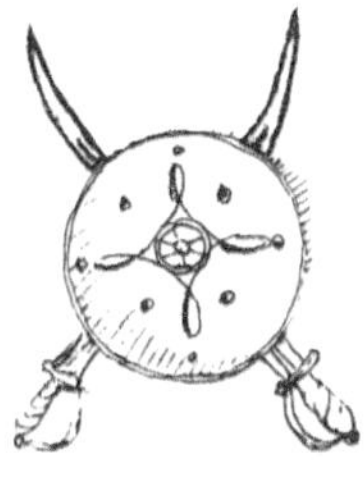

The Pandit and the Wodeyar's father had been good friends from his childhood.

Once Vishalaksha Pandit had studied the Wodeyar's horoscope and the lines on his palm and declared, "Annaji, you will be a raja one day."

True, the Wodeyars were related to the Arasus, the Mysore rulers, but there was no reason for anyone to suppose that the boy would ever become raja. Everyone in the family was pleased with the Pandit's prediction, but no one took it seriously.

Vishalaksha Pandit did not say anything more. He drew the boy close to him and said, "Remember, you must have a sense of commitment to whatever you undertake. You must learn horse-riding and sword-fighting. If ever you become a raja you must be determined to rule the land wisely. And you should appoint me minister. Do you agree, annayya?" The boy kept saying Hn, hn, to everything the Pandit said, thinking it was all in jest.

A few years later, it seemed as if the Pandit's words were coming true. But the throne went to one of Chikkadevaraja's cousins on that occasion. After a few years, however, he did become the raja. He remembered the Pandit's words and made him the chief minister.

Chikkadevaraja Wodeyar is justly famous in history as an able ruler who brought recognition for the state of Mysore from the Mughal Emperor. Realising that for the development of the state, the royal treasury must be full, he made a great effort to keep the revenue flowing in steadily. And during his reign, it became a flood. So the Wodeyar was able to provide for his people, the kind of facilities in agriculture and transport that one could not have imagined in those days. In these projects, he had the guidance of Vishalaksha Pandit, whose sharp intelligence helped him to make the right decisions in all matters.

The Pandit had no family of his own. Besides the affairs of the state, he had no other interests. Advising the Raja, playing chess with him, reading when he had the leisure – this was his life. The Raja had a special love and regard for the Pandit, who had given him ungrudging love, ever since he was a boy. They shared a deep affection and had great trust in each other.

The Raja had another minister, Tirumalarya, whose family had been in the royal service for many generations. He too was an able administrator. If the Pandit had not come from Chamarajanagar to become the chief minister, Tirumalarya would definitely have been one of the persons considered for that office. Tirumalarya served in the Pandit's cabinet along with Narasimha Shastry and Padmarasa Pandit who, like himself, had been in the Raja's service for a long time.

When the Wodeyar came to power, he tightened up the procedures for collecting taxes, so the people in some parts of the state suffered great hardships. Until then, many of them used to evade taxes by bribing the local officials. They could no longer do that. Some rebelled against the administration, not knowing how strict the Raja could be in such matters. It was believed that the Jangamas had encouraged the rebels. The Raja himself led the army to suppress the rebellion and captured the leaders. He then arranged a meeting to listen to their grievances. Many of the Jangamas were severely punished. In imposing this punishment, Vishalaksha Pandit was found to be harsher than the Raja. As a result, rumours spread, that because the Pandit was a Jain, he was taking revenge on the Veerashaivas, with whom he had an old enmity. All the ministers were in agreement with the Raja's decision, but it was Vishalaksha Pandit's reputation that suffered. It was said that the Veerashaivas had made up their minds to pay him back for what he had done to the Jangamas.

The Pandit was not one to be cowed down by such threats. He believed that anything that happened was predetermined. Like a man who has firm faith that God will take care of him, he was at peace with himself. Whenever any well-wisher told him to be careful, he would say with a smile, "I have not done anything wrong. Anyway, what can we do to an enemy? God is there to look after us."

Generally, the ministers and the chief minister were in agreement on matters of state administration. But when disputes arose over caste or religion, they would sit together, discuss the issue and arrive at a consensus. Sometimes, Vishalaksha Pandit would take a decision on his own, inform the others, and after he had the Raja's approval, act on it. On one such occasion, the Pandit and Tirumalarya could not see eye to eye.

There was a village in the district of Belur which had, for a long time, been accredited to the Chennakeshava temple in Belur. The Jains of the Parshvanatha temple in Halebid claimed that their temple had a hereditary right to it, so the village should be returned to them. Probably sometime in the past, it had been taken away from them and handed over to the Vaishnavas. Matters had remained like that until Vishalaksha Pandit became the chief minister. Then the Jains became more hopeful and pressed their claim to the village. It so happened that a Jain, by the name of Bucchanna, was appointed the overlord of the district of Halebid. He investigated this matter and decided that the village was, rightfully, the property of the Jain temple. He submitted a memorandum to the Raja, recommending that it should be restored to the Jains. Thus it was taken away from the Vaishnavas. Tirumalarya knew that the memorandum had been received. But the Pandit had not asked him to participate in the debate on it, and so, he was upset. Then the people who had lost the village, came to the capital. They wanted Tirumalarya to arrange an audience with the Raja, so that they could submit their petition. Tirumalarya went to the Raja with their request and arranged a meeting for them, one afternoon.

As the Raja took his place, he had Vishalaksha Pandit and

Narasimha Shastry on one side and Tirumalarya and Padmarasa Pandit on the other. In front of him stood the four Vaishnavas, ready to submit their appeal. The Raja turned to Vishalaksha Pandit and asked, "Do you know what their plea is, Panditare?"

"I understand they have come with a request to the mahaswami about Irulapura village. I do not know the details. If they are permitted to speak, mahaswami can hear about it and we too will come to know what it is," the Pandit said.

"Speak," the Raja ordered the Vaishnavas.

Tirumalarya told the group, "Present your appeal before the mahaswami."

"Mahaswami, lrulapura has belonged to our temple since time immemorial. Recently, Bucchana, the Jain sarvadhikari, has started giving us some trouble. The Jains raised the matter that the village had been legally made over to the Parshvanatha temple. They got a memorandum prepared, held some kind of an enquiry and decided that it must be restored to them. They submitted their claim and obtained the mahaswami's consent to it.

"We are all workers in the Chennakeshava temple. The Lord's service is possible only with the income from the village. Our lives too depend on it. If the village is taken away from us, the main source of revenue will be lost to the temple. Our food will go to someone else. Taking away that which belongs to God or his servants, is not good for the state. It is inauspicious for the mahaswami too. We have come here to place the facts before our mahaswami and ask him to reverse the decision made earlier, thereby restoring the traditional service to God and ensuring our own survival. Listen to our fervent plea and return the village to the temple in Belur, mahaswami," he said.

"When did all this take place, Panditare?" the Raja wanted to know.

"I brought this matter to your notice some three months ago, mahaswami," Vishalaksha Pandit replied. "The local officers were informed of your decision later. Both Shastry and Padmarasa Pandit were present when the matter was discussed."

"Why was Tirumalarya not present on that occasion?"

"Because he had been unwell for three days."

"What can we do about it now? The decision was taken after giving the matter much thought. It must stand."

"If your decision stays mahaswami, we, the poor people, will be ruined," the appellants pleaded.

"It is either you or they who will be destroyed," the Raja replied. "Both of you cannot lay claim to the same village"

Tirumalarya came in at that juncture. "Mahaswami must understand the implications of what the appellants are saying. The property which belonged to a particular temple has been taken away and handed over to another. It's like snatching away their food and giving it to someone else."

"We have looked into all that, Tirumalarya," Vishalaksha Pandit intervened. "The village belonged to the Parshvanatha temple a hundred years ago. A Srivaishnava officer is said to have handed it over to the temple in Belur at that time. Even now, there are some people who remember hearing that the village was the property of the Parshvanatha temple, when they were children. There is also a record in the book of accounts to say that the income from the village went to that temple. There is no such entry in the book to establish that the Belur temple received the revenue from it before that time. We took all this into account before this decision was recommended to the Raja."

He then turned to the appellants and asked, "Is there any evidence in your temple's accounts to prove that a hundred years ago, the income from the village went to it?"

"There is, swami. We can show it to you," they replied.

"Yes, it is not difficult for a clever person to produce proof and even swear by it," said Vishalaksha Pandit.

Tirumalarya interrupted, "Panditare, not only did you take away the livelihood of these wretched people, you are now accusing them of manufacturing evidence to support their claim! You are a great man. Why should you talk like this?"

"I am not being unfair to them. I know that such things have happened in many cases. How often have you and I discussed it. You yourself have told me how, when the Srivaishnavas were powerful, they had taken away the property of the Jain temples and attached it to their own," Vishalaksha Pandit replied.

Tirumalarya turned to the Raja. "This should not become a debate between the Pandit and me. Mahaswami is responsible for enforcing dharma in the state. Is it right to take away property from the Srivaishnavas, now, and hand it over to the Jains, just because someone in the past had taken it away from the Jains and given it to the Srivaishnavas? Besides, we have only been hearing about it for ages, There is no way of knowing what really happened at that time. So is it proper for us to perform 'an act of injustice now to set right one committed in the past?"

It was the turn of Padmarasa Pandit. "Mahaswami, where's the doubt? By just looking at what they call a Srivaishnava temple now, you can tell that it was a Jain temple in the past. Not only did the Srivaishnavas take away the Jain property, they also installed the idol of Vishnu in the temples and converted them into Vaishnava ones. They threw the Jain idols out on to the streets."

"Perhaps they thought, a god who wears no clothes, what does he need a house for?" the Raja laughed.

"Mahaswami, these poor men have come before you with their troubles, in the hope of being given some solution. Instead of doing that, our Pandit has started a discussion about philosophy. Even if all his arguments are valid, they have nothing do with their appeal. Besides in such cases, it is difficult to establish the truth. Which Srivaishnava temple was a Jain one in the past? What evidence has he to say such things?"

"Don't your own people grant that the Janardana temple in the important town of Mandya, was once a Jain temple?" Padmarasa Pandit countered.

"Our people say all sorts of things," Tirumalarya replied. "They have no idea of what will enhance their reputation or what will damage it. And whatever they might say in their ignorance, should people like you, who know better, believe them? Only a fool is proud to make such claims.

"Anyway, what is meant by saying that a Jain temple was converted into a Vaishnava one? There are many among us who take pride in saying that in the past, our acharyas used to crush five hundred Jains in the stone-mill on any given day. These same people also maintain that our acharyas were men of great compassion. We shouldn't attach any importance to such senseless words."

Vishalaksha Pandit came in at that point. "We seem to be straying away from the matter on hand. I have been impartial while considering the question of this village. I am convinced that the Jain temple had a claim over it in the past. That is why I submitted the report of the sarvadhikari to mahaswami with my recommendation."

"If I were to examine the evidence that you looked into before making your decision, I too should reach the same conclusion, shouldn't I?" asked Tirumalarya.

"How can one say that? It all depends upon one's point of view," Vishalaksha Pandit replied.

"Why, is it an instance of pure knowledge?" said Tirumalarya.

"I am a little older than you, Tirumalarya. I have great regard for you. But you seem to be forgetting all that and speaking disrespectfully to me." Vishalaksha Pandit was annoyed.

The Raja could not see the cause for the Pandit's anger. "What did you say, Tirumalarya?" he wanted to know.

"Mahaswami, in the Pandit's philosophical system, ultimate knowledge is that which comes naturally to any living being. And some worthy souls are able to divine the real nature of things, without even looking at them. I referred to his reaching a conclusion without any evidence as pure knowledge. That is why he took offence."

The Raja was surprised and amused. "Why should you get upset by that, Panditare? Say something about his Vishishtadvaita, if you like."

"He has commented on it several times, mahaswami," Tirumalarya said. "Our faith, according to him, is like the light on a dividing wall. We do not have the courage to call it either Dvaita or Advaita. And so, we call it Vishistadvaita and walk with our faces turned in both directions."

"That was meant as a joke!" Padmarasa Pandit cut in. "You too have made fun of the Jain faith. But your words today were very harsh."

The Raja was wondering how he could settle their dispute. If he could bring up a non-controversial topic, then he might be able to pacify them, and make them give up their confrontational attitude. Turning to Padmarasa Pandit, he said, "Tell me. What else has Tirumalarya said about the Jain faith?"

"The basis of our faith, as mahaswami knows, is the assertion of possibility. Tirumalarya uses that as an argument to maintain that ours is a cowardly faith compared to Vishishtadvaita. According to him, we respond to anything with, It is possible. Even if someone said our father is a woman, our faith will not permit us to say No, he is not."

It was Vishalaksha Pandit's turn. "These words, apparently spoken in jest, often hide a real feeling of aversion. Our own people, in the past, gave up their faith to become Srivaishnavas. Now, their descendants are belittling the faith of their forefathers."

Tirumalarya was furious. He stood up. "Mahaswami, the Pandit has called me a descendant of a Jain in your august presence. I cannot imagine anything more insulting than this. Kindly permit me to leave. I will return to the service of the court later. But I will not tolerate this blasphemy ... this profanity against God, the Bhagavata and the

Acharyas. Why should I stay here any longer?" Saying this, he did a namaskara before the Raja and got ready to leave.

"Why are you so angry?" asked Vishalaksha Pandit. "I didn't say you were of Jain descent. Do sit down."

When Tirumalarya took his seat, Vishalaksha Pandit turned to the Raja. "I think Mahaswami must reconsider this matter. It seems that one evening, eight days ago, our Srivaishnava subjects, unhappy at the loss of their village, caught hold of the officer Bucchanna when he was alone and beat him up. I hadn't anticipated so much trouble."

The leader of the appellants spoke up at once. "Mahaswami, we are not the kind to beat up anyone. Some youngsters among us started talking wildly about what they would do. We kept them in check. It is true that the officer was beaten up a few days later. But his behaviour was not blameless. It is said that he molested a married woman, and so her people beat him up. Our boys might have let their tongues run, but they would not assault an officer. Why, a couple of them even threatened to come to Mysore to beat up the chief minister. That doesn't mean anything."

"So one thing led to another, didn't it?"

"The Jangama rose in revolt on the question of tax. Now the Srivaishnava rebels for a piece of land. That's all," said the Pandit.

Tirumalarya was once again provoked by the remark. "What are you saying, Panditare, in the presence of the Raja? How can you equate these poor souls, who have come to beg the Raja for a favour, with the Jangamas who revolted against the state?" He turned to the Raja, "Mahaswami, I arranged this audience for these poor brahmins because they said they had a submission to make to you. You have given them a learing. Now, whatever directive the mahaswami considers just, it will be accepted. I am very upset by what has transpired here. If I remain here any longer, I am likely to say some rude words and hear a few in return. I don't want that. I'll come back tomorrow to be at your service." He took leave of the Raja with folded hands and left the place.

The Raja addressed the appellants. "Let us see. It may not be possible to return the village to you. We will arrange to have another piece of land transferred to you."

After they went away, he told Shastry and Padmarasa that they too could go home. Then he went into the inner chamber with Vishalaksha Pandit for a game of chess.

It was very late in the night by the time the game ended. As Vishalaksha Pandit stood up to leave, the Raja called a servant and asked if there was a torch-bearer to go with the Pandit. The man replied that there was.

"Let a body-guard also accompany him," the Raja ordered.

"That is not necessary, prabhu," the Pandit said. "If you need me, I will come."

"Why not? You have many enemies as it is and now, these Vaishnavas from Iralapura."

"Poor things! They aren't the type to attack anyone. They just blurt out something when they are angry. There is no rancour in their hearts, just the grief of losing their livelihood. Once mahaswami gives them another village, the problem will be solved. Both are our subjects. If either goes hungry, it is as if our own children are starving."

"So why did you take away their village, then?" the Raja asked.

"Someone in the past deprived the Jains of what was theirs and gave it to the Vaishnavas. Mahaswami considered it unjust and restored it to the rightful owners."

The Raja laughed. The Pandit went home.

Even as the Raja went into his private chambers to take off his coat and change into freshly washed clothes, an attendant entered and in a voice trembling with fear, said, "Mahaswami, the Pandit has been attacked by some murderers it seems."

"Where? What happened?" the Raja exclaimed.

Vishalaksha Pandit lived on the first floor of a house on a street near the north gate of the fort. To reach the place, one had to walk along a narrow lane. There were many such lanes near the houses there. As the Pandit was making his way home, with the torch-bearer in front and the bodyguard behind him, someone jumped on him from the verandah of an empty house, and rained blows on his head and back. With a cry, the Pandit fell down. The attackers fled before the guard realised what was happening. People rushed out of their homes on hearing the Pandit's cry. Blood was streaming from the Pandit's head. His back and rib-cage were broken. He called the bodyguard. "Inform the Raja and take me home," he told him.

It has been mentioned earlier that the Raja had great regard and affection for the Pandit. The Raja's first thought was to catch hold of the assassins and put them to death. He was also very anxious to see the Pandit. He put on his coat, called for the servants, sent for the vaidya and asked everyone to go to the Pandit's residence. The Raja reached the place within ten minutes and sat by the Pandit's bed.

Seeing his Raja, Vishalaksha Pandit made an effort to sit up. "Should you bother about showing us respect even when you are lying there hurt and helpless?" said the Raja and gently pushed him back on to the bed. Then he asked what had happened.

The Pandit's words came haltingly. "My journey here has come to an end. I must take leave of you. I thought that our meeting in the palace would be the last one. But the compassionate mahaprabhu was good enough to come here. I am happy I could have another glimpse of his face."

The Raja's eyes filled with tears. The Pandit gestured that he was in excruciating pain. Softly, the Raja asked him, "Who was it? Anyone from Tirumalaryav's side?" the Raja asked.

The Pandit's eyes opened wide. "No, no," he said. The Raja fell silent.

After a pause the Pandit spoke again. "The one thing I wanted, ever since you were a child, was your well-being. I served you to the best of my ability and you looked after me well. Rajyalakshmi, the Goddess of Fortune, has blessed you. You will handle her carefully. I have no reason to worry about the state. But the Raja cannot look after everything. A competent chief minister is essential. If I had lived longer, I would have raised your glory to greater heights. But this was all the service that was granted to me. There's no use thinking about it. But I want you to promise me something. I'll die in peace if you do it."

The words stuck in the Raja's throat. "I will certainly do it. I promise," he said in a choked voice.

There was a pause. Again the Raja asked, "What is it, Panditare?"

"When mahaswami came to the throne and made me the chief minister, many people were unhappy. Once I shut my eyes, there will be many among the elders who will want to be considered for the position. The Raja should not appoint anybody who comes. He should select the one who deserves to be in the post. If you give me your promise, I'll name the man who is worthy of becoming your chief minister."

"Tell me the name first. Then you will have my answer," the Raja said.

The Pandit drew a deep breath. "At present, there is no one in the Arasu family that is in your service, who is competent enough for that post. They are completely loyal, but in a minister that is not enough. The same is true of my other colleagues. The only one who is suitable in all respects is," he paused, then added,

"Tirumalarya."

The Raja was astounded. "Only this afternoon you had a serious disagreement with him. What is this you are saying now?"

"That is a different matter. I stated what I thought was right. So did he. But neither of us said anything that was obviously unfair. He is the only who will ensure that there is justice in everything and thereby guarantee the Raja's peace of mind. If you promise to make him the chief minister, I will gladly surrender this body."

"I had expected you to suggest Padmarasa's name," the Raja said.

"He is an honest man. Let him be there to help Tirumalarya. He cannot manage the chief ministership."

"You are truly magnanimous. I knew you were a noble soul. It's only now that I have understood how noble."

"I am grateful this will be carried out. If you can send for Tirumalarya, I would like to see him once more. Just like water flows out of a pot with a hole in it, life seems to be draining away from this body."

Even as someone standing nearby was about to send a messenger, Tirumalarya's voice was heard near the door. He rushed into the room asking, "How is he? Is he hurt badly?" but lowered his voice on seeing the Raja.

"Namaskara, mahaswami," he said before coming to the bedside. "How unlucky can we be! That this should happen the same day those rascals threatened to beat you up. It must have been an inauspicious hour when they spoke ... How are you? Where have you been hurt?" he enquired in a gentle voice,

The Pandit signalled to Tirumalarya to come to the left of his bed. He took Tirumalarya's hands and pressed them to his eyes, then drew his head close to his own. "I don't have long to live. I have already spoken to the Raja. You must take my place and be the chief minister. I always feared for the Raja's life. But that evil has now befallen me. Take good care of him. I take your leave."

Tirumalarya was lost for words. "I don't know what your feelings about me are, at this moment. I offended you with my words this afternoon. People may even think that I was behind the attack on you."

Vishalaksha Pandit put his hand on Tirumalarya's mouth. "You shouldn't be saying such things. Anger is for the living. What need I have for it now? Don't I know your qualities? Not one bad habit. I have often told the Raja that chess is my one weakness, but Tirumalarya isn't guilty even of that. He spends his free time reading ... Give me your word ..."

Tirumalarya said, "I will never go against the Raja's orders."

Vishalaksha Pandit smiled weakly and lay back in peace. The had, in the meantime, bandaged the wounds to stop the bleeding and given him some medicine to steady the pulse. But it of no use.

The Raja asked, "Do you have any other wishes ? Would you like to meet the acharya or an elder from your math?"

The Pandit replied, "Of what use is the math to me now? My is going back to where it came from. Who can change its course?"

He stretched out his limbs and closed his eyes. Within a minute or of that, he passed away.

"Perhaps he might have carried on a little longer if we hadn't him speak so much," said the Raja. "He was like an uncle to and I have lost him now. He has shifted the load he was carrying to you, Tirumalarya. Did he tell you that?"

Tirumalarya replied, "Yes, he did. I am at the Raja's command."

Silently, both of them came to the door. Then the Raja whispered Tirumalarya, "I don't understand it. Did he become an atheist in end?"

"Mahaswami, many people are believers in their speech, but their actions. Vishalaksha Pandit's words might have been of an atheist but his entire life affirmed the existence of God. We would't find a greater believer than the Pandit."

The arrangements for the Pandit's funeral rites were supervised by Tirumalarya. The Raja appointed him the chief minister, thus carrying out the Pandit's last wish. No one, either in the cabinet or the royal household, was unhappy about it, as everyone had known Tirumalarya for years.

Tirumalarya carried out the decision made by the Pandit regarding the dispute. The temple in Belur was bequeathed another village instead of Irulapura.

Mangamma The Curd-Seller

Mangamma has been supplying curds to our family as a matter of routine, for several years. The arrangement we have is peculiar to Bangalore. In other places, the tradition is that every day without fail, the curds is brought to the house and money for it is collected at the end of the month. I do not think that such a practice exists in Bangalore. Whenever

Mangamma passed by our locality, she would come to our house and ask if we needed the excellent curds she had brought. If we did, we would take some and pay her then and there, at the prevailing market rate. Sometimes we paid the following day. This was the arrangement we had with her.

Mangamma came from a village near Avaluru with a name like Venkatapura or something. She had to pass our locality on her way to the town. Perhaps because I spoke nicely to her, Mangamma invariably stopped at our house either while going into the town or on her way home. She would sit for a while in the courtyard, put a betel leaf and nut into her mouth, or ask us for it if she did not have any, and chat with us. If I had some time on my hands, she would tell me all about her joys and sorrows, and ask me to talk about mine. What problems did I have! God has been good to us. Not having much to say, I would tell her about ordinary household matters, how the cat had drunk all the milk, or that a rat had eaten the pumpkin, and that was enough. Mangamma, with the wisdom gained from experience, would say that is how the world is, and then launch into a lesson on how to run it. All said and done, I must say that I was very fond of her and there was a trusting relationship between us.

About a month ago, early one morning, Mangamma called out, asking if we needed curds. I was somewhere inside, so my son said, Yes, and went up to her with his hand stretched out. Mangamma took a ladleful of creamy curds from the pot and gave it to him saying, "Go tell your mother to come soon. I have to go." I came out just then.

"You have given birth to a piece of pure gold in that boy, amma. He has the same qualities you have. But what does it all come to? It lasts only till they grow up. Then, some girl comes along and the son, who goes Amma, Amma, all the time now, will not even bother to ask if you are dead or alive."

"What is the matter, Mangamma?" I asked. "Did your son disobey you?"

"What can I say, amma? Why should I expect my boy to listen to me, when the man who took my hand didn't heed my words?"

"What's this about your husband, Mangamma? What happened'" I asked.

"Ayyo, amma! I didn't go about in a good saree. Some other woman did. Attracted by the saree, he went after her. Never mind. I didn't say anything because I wanted him to feel that he had a home and wife to come back to. Because I sold amritha which I shouldn't have, I lost my husband. That was my fate. But you better take care, amma. Make sure you are in a nice saree when your husband comes home. Men's minds are very fickle, remember. You should make sure their eyes are on you by wearing an attractive saree or a blouse. To keep them happy, put flowers in your hair, use attar. This saree you have on now is all right while you are by yourself, doing the housework. You must change into a good one in the evening."

I was amused by these words, although I realised that they were wise words, which came from her own experience. I also felt sorry that she had got hurt while acquiring that wisdom. "You are right, Mangamma," I said to her.

She went on, "Amma, there are four ways of holding a man. Some people will advise you to feed him this root or that herb. You may as well send him straight to the grave. Don't listen to them. Instead, cook a dish that tastes good to his tongue, dress well so that you please his eyes, and no matter if you are unhappy or ill, have a smile on your face. Buy a sufficient quantity of all the things you need so that you don't bother him frequently. Save a few paise here and a few paise there, so that you can offer him a rupee or two when he needs money. This is the root and herb that will work. If the woman of the house does this, the man will stay like a pet dog. If not, he will take to the streets." I was surprised by the unexpectedness of what she said. After a few more words, I sent her off.

When Mangamma came to our place a fortnight ago, she seemed to be particularly upset. "What's the matter, Mangamma? Why are you looking like this?" I enquired.

"What can I say, amma? Nobody wants me anymore," she replied, wiping her eyes with the end of her sari.

"What happened? Did your son say something to you?" I asked.

"Yes," she said. "I don't know what the little one did, but his mother was beating hint. I couldn't bear it, so I said, What's wrong with you, woman, you are hitting the child like a rakshasi! She said all sorts of things to me, amma! So I said, How can you talk to me, your husband's own mother, like this? Let's see what he has to say. Well, when the maharaya came home, I told him, Look, your wife punishes the child for nothing. She abuses me when I tell her to stop. Why don't you talk to her, put some sense into her? Talk to me, she shouted. Don't I have the right to scold him if he does something wrong? Haven't I given birth to him, just as you gave birth to my husband? I don't need anyone's advice ... After all, amma, she is his wife. I'm only his mother She turns on me if I say anything, but I can't do the same, can I? You know what my son said? He Said, Yes Avva, if she beats her own child, why should you bother? Punish me, if you like . "Why? Was I wrong in what I said, I asked him. I don't know whether it's right or wrong. But we must grant her the right to punish her own child, he said ... I was furious, amma, and didn't know what I was saying. What's this, son? I asked him. You are so much under her spell that you find nothing wrong if she beats the child or tells me to keep quiet. I wouldn't be surprised if you drive me out tomorrow, because she asks you to ... Do you know what he said amma? ... What do you expect me to do, if you say you won't stay here with her ... she is a helpless woman. What about me, am I not helpless? I asked him. Avva, you have everything, you have cattle, you have your money, I don't have to look after you ... When I asked if he really wanted me to live separately, his reply was ... It's your wish Avva. I won't stop you, if that's what you want. I've had enough of this quarrelling. All right, then. I am on my own from this afternoon, I told him. Be happy with your wife ... I left after that with the curds, amma."

Mangamma started crying and I tried to console her. "It's not a big thing, Mangamma. You wait and see. I know what's going to happen. You will go back and everything will be as before, believe me." I bought some curds, and Mangamma went away.

When she came the next day, she seemed a little more composed though she was not her usual, cheerful self. "Mangamma, I am sure everything has been sorted out," I said.

"No hope of that, amma. Do you think that daughter-in-law of mine will allow mother and son to be on good terms? By the time I went back home, she had put all my pots and pans to one side. In one gudan there was ragi, in another, rice, some salt, chillies, everything. She and her husband had had their food, and she was sitting there, with her legs stretched out. How can anything be sorted out like this, amma? I had to cook some ragi flour for myself. I know they were waiting for me to give them an excuse to throw me out. Is your son your own, once he is married? Why should I force myself on them, when my own son doesn't want me? I'm all alone now, amma. Every day, I used to give some curds to the child before setting out on my rounds. This morning, just as I was leaving, she took him out. I know she doesn't want me to talk to the child."

I was shocked that this trivial matter had been blown up to such proportions. But there was nothing that I could do. After I had said a few words to her, she went away.

The subject did not come up over the next few days. It was my impression that Mangamma was living separately from her family. One day she asked me, "Amma, that velvet blouse you wear, how much is it for a yard?"

"Why, Mangamma?"

"All this while, I was putting aside some money for my son and my grandson, amma. Why should I do it now? I'll get a velvet blouse for myself."

"It may cost seven, eight rupees, Mangamma," I said.

That very day, Mangamma bought the velvet cloth, took it to the tailor and asked him to make a blouse for her. She was wearing it the next day, on her way home.

"Do you see me, amma, all dressed up? When my husband was with me, I didn't buy a good saree, and he went after another woman. I saved money for my son, and look what happened. But now, see, I'm all decked up."

Mangamma was no longer herself. Must be the shock of losing her son, I thought. Extreme anger could do that to anyone. I did not make any comments.

But that velvet blouse of hers landed her in trouble with others. There was a boy from her village who was studying in Bangalore. He was a dandy, who went about dressed like a European, or like our educated people with tie, collar and all. He saw Mangamma and made fun of her, saying, "What's all this, Mangamma, you are wearing a velvet blouse?"

"Watch your tongue, fellow," Mangamma retorted. "If you can go about with a noose round your neck, why can't I wear a velvet blouse ?" Words were exchanged between them and there was much laughter among the onlookers.

I heard about this incident from Mangamma the next day. Not only the others, even her own daughter-in-law had said, in Mangamma's hearing, "She doesn't buy her daughter-in-law a piece of cloth, but now, sets up her own house and flaunts a velvet blouse"

At the wedding, Mangamma had given her daughter-in-law a necklace, earrings, bangles, pendants and a waist band. Even after that, once a year, she bought her some piece of jewellery. But the girl had forgotten all that. Mangamma had kept quiet the first couple of times her daughter-in-law had made such remarks. Then she could not bear it any longer. She went to her son one night, and said, Your wife has been making all sorts of remarks about me, just because I had a blouse made. I have not given her anything, she claims. Are all those bangles, earrings, jewellery, nothing? The girl did not allow her husband to speak. You are an old woman without a husband, you want to wear earrings and a gold belt round your waist? Here. Take them. Put them on she said. Enough of this talk, woman, the son silenced her and turned to his mother. Look, Avva, I do not want to get involved in your quarrel. If you want your jewels, take them back.

Mangamma was very bitter. "Look, amma, the fellow doesn't bother to tell his wife not to say such things in the presence of outsiders. Instead, he asks me to take back the jewels, as if I am to blame in the matter ... Enough, amma. I have had enough of this life." When I heard all this, I felt very sorry for Mangamma. She was an old woman. He was her only son. Why could his wife not look after him and his mother? All this fuss was because the old woman had said, Don't beat the child. I wondered why people behaved like this with one another. And then it occurred to me that most quarrels start this way. Because two people do not get on with each other, a trivial incident gets blown up. A bitter quarrel follows, resulting in endless pain for everyone concerned.

A few days later, Mangamma said to me, "Amma, you are a good person. I have some money with me. Will you keep it safe, in that place they call the bank or something? There are some people who have their eyes on it." I asked her what had happened.

"There's a fellow in our village called Rangappa, amma. One of those who likes a good life, gambles a little once in a while. Yesterday as I was coming along with my pot of curds, he appeared from somewhere. How are you, Mangamma? he asked. If this is what you think is all right, then I'm all right, I told him. That's true, he agreed, adding, With the way things are these days, who can be happy? Youngsters will answer rudely and old timers like us will wonder what all this is and bear it, he said.

"We walked along till we reached the well in the grove. I was nervous, wondering what he would do. I had some money in my pouch. But nothing happened. He only asked for some chunam. I gave it to him. Then he went away. Today, he was there again, amma. After talking abut this and that, he said, Mangamma, I'm badly in need of some money. Will you lend it to me? I will return it as soon as I sell my ragi crop. Where do I have any money, I asked him. Come on, Mangamma, we all know you have it. There's no use keeping it hidden here and there, he said. Give me a loan. You can save me, and at the same time, earn some interest. After a while he added, I wouldn't have asked you if you were still living with your son. Then you might have wanted to get some jewellery made for your daughter-in-law. Now there is no need for that, is there, he said.

"See amma, this is what happens if a woman is all by herself. People get all sorts of ideas," she said. I told her I would consult my husband and let her know.

I had not talked to my husband about it by the time Mangamma came the next day. After having given us our supply of curds, she took out a pouch that was tucked into her waist. "Amma, let's go in," she said. "You can count the money."

I told her that I had not discussed it with my husband and suggested that she could bring the money later. "I'm frightened, amma," she said. "Rangappa was there again today. We were in the grove and he said, Sit down, Mangamma, what's the hurry? I had this money with me, so my heart started thudding. What if I refused? Suppose he forcibly stopped me? I was afraid, so I sat down. He talked of this and that. Then holding my hand, he said, Mangamma, you are so beautiful ... Did you hear that, amma. The man who had taken my hand when I was still young, left me. No one had held it until now, and this fellow ... I pulled my hand away and said, What's this, Rangappa? You are fooling with me? Are you my husband to talk about my looks?

"I walked away quickly from there, amma. Yesterday he was after my money, today he was after my honour. My husband, the man who sat beside me on the decorated seat, with a basinga tied on his head, went his way. He left me in the prime of youth. Another person in my place would have willingly looked for a chance for happiness elsewhere. I decided not to, for the sake of my honour. And today this rascal comes along to hold my hand ..."

I felt that the matter had taken a serious turn. "Look, Mangamma, it's not worth all this bother. Why don't you forget what happened and go back to your son?" I advised.

"You know I'm willing, amma. But that woman ..."

"Tell your son all this."

"Ayyo, amma, she will make a scene and drive me out of the community! It's getting late. I'd better go. Speak to your husband and let me know tomorrow, amma," she said.

She came back within an hour. "Amma, something happened."

"What?"

"I had bought some mithai for the child and kept it in my basket ..."

I did not know who she was referring to.

"Which child?" I asked.

"My grandchild, of course."

"But you told me he wasn't allowed to talk to you?"

"That's what the mother says. Do you think the child stays away? He comes to me when she isn't looking, drinks the milk I keep aside for him and asks for curds. You should see him jumping with joy whenever I give him something. When he throws a tantrum, I tell him his mother will come to take him away. Immediately, he keeps quiet.

What games children think at, amma! Today I had bought some mithai for him. I had it in the basket. Do you know what happened as I was coming through Shankarapura? A crow sitting on a mango tree came swooping down and took away the packet. Such a thing had to happen today of all days," she moaned.

"Its only a packet of mithai, Mangamma. You can buy some more."

"That's not it, amma," she wailed. "They say a crow must not touch a human being."

"Why? What if it touches you?"

"They say it's a threat to your life. I thought for a minute that my end was near and I was frightened. But the very next moment, I was happy that I was going. A life no one wanted, or needed. I'm better off at His feet, I told myself."

"What nonsense!" I exclaimed. "You keep a packet of sweets where any crow can get it, and then you say it's a sign of your death! Are these wise words, Mangamma? Go home quietly."

"There's nothing to fear, then?"

"No fear, no danger, nothing. Haven't you heard it said that one's life-span increases with each quarrel? Forget about the whole thing and go home with a smile."

I kept thinking about her after she had gone. The way her mind worked was strange. She wanted to be with her son, her daughter-in-law and her grandchild. But she also wanted them to respect her as the head of her household. It is natural for a human being to feel that way, I thought. One may be troubled by all sorts of worries in life, yet one does not want to die because of them. Nor does one want to admit it. Innocent and simple village folk, no trace of deceit in them – how true was that belief? Layer beneath layer and fold within fold, even in their lives. Who can fathom this strange thing called life, I wondered.

Mangamma came with another piece of news on her next visit. The child would not leave her and go back to his parents. She was very pleased about it. "Look at his courage, amma. He is not even this high, imagine leaving his mother! He came to me yesterday afternoon and refused to go back. All these days, he used to come on the sly. When he refused to go back, his mother screamed and shouted and threatened to thrash him. He clung to my knees and said he wasn't going. I tried to send him back. His father too coaxed him. But no, he wouldn't budge. Wouldn't let go of me, amma. Ever since I started living by myself, ten days ago, I was a little nervous at night, sleeping alone. Last night, with the child there, I got some confidence. After all, he is a man, isn't he? God must have put it into his little head, that's why when my grown-up son left me, this little one came, as if to say, Don't worry, I'm with you.

"My daughter-in-law ranted through the night, but he wouldn't leave my side. Because I didn't want him to be alone during the day, I left him at his mother's door before I set out this morning. He went in and I came here, amma."

"What will you do if his mother beats him?"

"No, she won't. She will be thrilled that her boy has come back for at least half a day. All that beating is only when he is with her all the time, I know. It's like this, amma. When we all stayed under the same roof, I never noticed how beautiful my daughter-in-law is. Now when I look at her from a distance, I realise it. May be not when she is angry. Otherwise, she's very good-looking. That's why my son is mad about her. It's the Same with him too. I never bothered about when he left for the fields or when he came back. Now I sit at my front door and worry if he is late and wonder why he has set out so early in the morning. She must be feeling the same about that child. If she beats him, he's sure to come with me in the morning when I leave on my rounds. She wouldn't want that, would she? She won't let the child she has carried for nine months and given birth to, go so easily."

[illegible] see how far ahead she could think. I was certain [illegible]ld be sorted out soon.

And that is exactly what happened. After two days with his mother, the child insisted on accompanying his grandmother to Bangalore. She couldn't possibly carry him in her arms, and the basket with the pot of curds on her head, as she walked the three miles to the city. She stood there not knowing what to do, when her son and daughter-in-law came up to her. Her son said, "Avva, something- happened. We made a mistake. But you also shouldn't get angry, should you" Some neighbours joined them and pacified her. And so it became possible for Mangamma to return to her family without any loss of face.

Then the child insisted on being with his grandmother all the time. So a new arrangement had to be made. All this while, Mangamma had kept the milk and curds business in her own hands. The reason given was that the daughter-in-law had to stay at home to manage the kitchen. But the real reason was that Mangamma would have some money of her own if she sold the milk and curds. When tlle child would not leave her, the daughter-in-law came to her and said, "Why should you go out in the hot sun, at your age? For how long will you do this work? As the head of the family, you stay at home and look after the kitchen. I'll attend to the curds business from now on."

Mangamma agreed. "All right, then. You take it over. And once in a while, I'll go."

One day, the two women came together. One had the child in her arms and the other carried the basket.

"Amma, this is my daughter-in-law. She didn't want to see an old woman cook her own food, so she took me back. She doesn't want me to go out in the sun either, and I agreed. So she will bring the curds for you from now on," Mangamma said and handed us over to her daughter-in-law.

I chatted with them for a while, advised them to live happily and peacefully, gave them both some betel leaves and nuts and sent them away.

It is the daughter-in-law who has been supplying us with curds since then. All this time, I had heard only Mangamma's side of the story, but I was curious about the girl's version. So one day I asked her, "You seem to be a sensible girl, Nanjamma. How could you drive your mother-in-law out of the house?"

"I'm not a rakshasi to do such a thing, amma. The problem is that she insisted on having her own way in everything. Should she forget that her son is the man of the house? What sort of a husband will he be, if he is forever his mother's boy? How can I run the home as a wife should? All right., she bore him, she brought him up. If she wants him, let her keep him, I said. If I beat my child, does she have the right to tell me not to? I protested as I had had enough, and stood up for my rights as the child's mother."

"But punishing the child is not how you show you are his mother, is it?"

"I may beat him, but I pet him too, amma. If you can say why are you beating him, you can as well say why are you fondling him! Amma, nothing is gained by trying to explain such things. That child is my son, and that son of hers is my husband. What sort of a life do I have if I can't say a word to my husband, and punish my child now and then? She should just let me be."

When I heard Mangamma's words, I thought she was right. Now, I felt this girl was right.

"So, do you have a little more independence at home now?" I asked.

"Much more than before, amma. One must adjust to the situation somehow. If I don't., and fight with her, someone or other is sure to swallow all her money. There's a fellow called Rangappa in our village. When she was living on her own, he asked her for a loan, it seems. And she had agreed to give it. He told me himself. That was when I told my child, Go to your ajji's house. She will give you mithai. Stay there only. Don't come back here until I tell you. I had to do it., so that our quarrel would end, amma."

"That means the child didn't go to his ajji on his own?"

"He wanted to. But I also made him go."

"Did you tell your husband you were going to do this?"

"Ayyo, does one say all these things, amma? Men don't understand them."

I realised that Nanjamma had as much commonsense as Mangamma. I am sure that the competition is still on in that household between Mangamma and her daughter-in-law, for the prize catch – the woman's son and the girl's husband. The mother is determined to not let him go and the wife bent on taking him away. It is something which goes on everywhere. No one can predict the outcome. The girl is like the crocodile who grabs the child by the leg under water, while the mother is on the bank, hanging on to his arm, determined to save him. In the midst of this, the plight of the child is a little difficult.

It is the same drama, whether it is in the house of Mangamma, the curd-seller from the village or in the house of Thangamma, who buys the curds from her.

A drama without the last act.

The Acharya's Wife

There is a place called Saligrama near Mirle Bherya in Mysore district. It must have been a big town in the past. It is not all that small even now. But is it possible to see again, the glory it had when the Hoysala kings reigned in Dwarasamudra? Now it looks as if the village does not realise its run-down state, lost as it is in the memories of its bygone glory. It stands there dumb,

like a school-boy who has forgotten his lesson, wondering who that great woman Sali could be, from whom it got its name. A gentle, eight-hundred-year-old light sleeps over the village, its tank, its fields, houses, streets, its temple and the pond with the mandapa by its side. It is in places like this, that Time brushes aside every other claim to greatness. Instead, it spreads its own grandeur like a covering cloth.

Eight hundred years ago, Ramanujacharya, the founder of the Vishishtadvaita school, lived here incognito, for a few years. He was born in Perumbudur, grew up in Kanchipura, and in Sriranga, he became an ascetic and propounder of Sri Vaishnava dharma. When there was a threat to his life from his enemies, at the insistence of his disciples he escaped into the land of the Hoysalas and lived there. A hallowed ground, it had once offered refuge to a group of mendicants, who had to flee their homes in the north when famine struck. Because of the abundant generosity of the land, the group survived and prospered. When the king in the southern region became a tyrant, those people who believed in dharma sought sanctuary here, like children who hide behind the uncle when their father is angry. The idol of Narasimhamurthy that the Acharya worshipped, is still there in the temple, an object of devotion. In one of the mandirs of the temple complex, there is a statue of the Acharya. So true to life is it, that you get the impression he is sitting there himself. In front is a pond. The people point to it and tell you, the Acharya used to wash here, and bathe here. As we listen to them and look at these precincts, it seems as if the wheels of time have slipped back eight hundred years, and we are now face to face with life in the age of the Hoysalas. There, look! An ascetic has stepped into the water. It is Ramanuja!

Ten years ago, I had gone to Saligrama. As I walked around the temple, I recalled the story of the Acharya. A wonderful tale. Of a boy, who was brought up in a poor family, who had extraordinary intelligence, had learnt about the Bhagavata dharma from five different gurus, and who went on to become the founder of a new school of thought. He earned for it, the respect of the king and by it, the souls of thousands were saved. I felt a sense of pride when I thought about the Acharya's life.

But one aspect of it troubled my mind. History tells us that it was mainly his wife's thoughtless behaviour that led him to renounce the world. Once, the Acharya wanted to honour his guru. His wife served him and then she took a bath because the guest was of a lower caste. Again, when there was an argument near the well, she spoke very rudely about the guru's family. Another time, she was lying in bed asleep, when the Acharya reached home late in the evening. This is why the Acharya decided to become an ascetic, they say. Perhaps what the Acharya did was right. But was not the punishment too great for her lapses?

The Acharya was full of learning and of his mission to serve dharma. Should he not have been a little more understanding and given the foolish woman some advice? Who knows what she was like! That is life. What had happened to her, after her husband left her to become an ascetic and she had gone back to her parents?

I sat there, under the tree, thinking. As I was watching a crane fly in to rest at the edge of the pond, a story was born.

After leaving the Chola land, Ramanujacharya reached the highlands of Mysore via Satyamangala. When they took one look at him, his disciples knew his enemies were at his heels. They did not allow him to wear his saffron robes and insisted that he should dress in white, while one of the disciples wore saffron. When the enemy king had sent for the Acharya a few days earlier, a disciple had gone to him, disguised as Ramanuja. The others had then led Ramanuja away to a place of safety in the north. There was some fear that he would be caught during the journey, so another of the disciples had dressed up as Ramanuja and was determined to surrender himself if someone came for the guru.

When they entered the Hoyasala kingdom, the disciples started looking for a place that was suitable for an ascetic. Then they came to Saligrama, they decided that it was the ideal place for the Acharya to settle in. Some of the disciples lived as sanyasis in distant villages, and came to meet their guru now and then. One of them stayed with the Acharya during the first fortnight. Later, he found that there was a man and his family in the village who would serve the master with devotion. So he handed over the task of taking care of the guru to them, and went away. There was no trace of the enemy from the south for over a year, so the fears of the Acharya's disciples gradually decreased. Two of them stayed behind in Tondanuru. The rest left for their hometowns with the understanding that news from those areas would be frequently dispatched to the guru.

The one who stayed behind in Saligrama to serve the Acharya is known in history as Vadaganambi, which means a devotee from the north. Vadaganambi was a brahmin of the Bhagavata tradition. As was the custom in those days, he had learnt Sanskrit, studied Vedanta, visited Kanchipura and Sriranga, and had become a recognised scholar. The privilege of worshipping the god Narasimha belonged exclusively to his family. When Vadaganambi heard that an ascetic had arrived there, he naturally wanted to be of service to him. He knew that the ascetic was old, but there were no signs of age either on his face or in his behaviour. And even though his body showed no signs of his years, there was no doubt that the knowledge he had was too great to be acquired in a single lifetime. Vadaganambi attended on the guru for three days. By then it was clear that the master belonged to the same Bhagavata tradition, so he asked the guru to accept him as a disciple. The Acharya agreed.

Vadaganambi's efforts to find out more about his guru came to nothing. He could not possibly ask the guru. The oilier disciple would not tell him anything either. So he did not pursue the matter. Besides, what was to be gained by knowing the details? The guru commanded respect, and that was enough. The Acharya was pleased with the rare humility that Vadaganambi displayed. The disciple from the south also was impressed. This quality brought Vadaganambi into the service of the guru in such a short time.

Vadaganambi's wonder grew day by day as he watched his guru's life. During a casual conversation, the guru had said he was eighty years old. For a man of eighty to be like this was astonishing, thought Vadaganambi. Even after he had spent all his time with the Acharya, for many days, he did not know when the guru retired for the night. Or when he woke up, since he would he up before Vadaganambi came to attend to his needs.

The guru did most things himself, rarely expecting any help. He would accept a little food the disciple had prepared as bhiksha in the presence of God and eat it at noon. At night he would be content with a glass of milk. The rest of the time he kept himself busy, either in meditation or in the service of God, or in reciting the texts he had studied. Vadaganambi was about forty years old. He had a wife, and a son who was six years old. He thought it was his good fortune that he had found a guru like the Acharya. So Vadaganambi asked his guru to let his wife and son serve him too. It was thus that Shamalambe and Ramachandra also became the Acharya's ardent disciples.

Two years passed in this manner.

In the meanwhile, Vadaganambi and his wife had come to know that the person they were looking after, their guru, was Ramanujacharya himself. Within a few days of their entering his service, the Acharya had told his disciples that these two, Shamalambe and Vadaganambi, who were taking such great care of him, must have been his daughter and son-in-law in a previous birth. Otherwise they would not be looking, after him as they did. He ordered his disciples to take the couple into their confidence and tell them everything. That was how the husband and wife came to know about the guru. Talking about the master's decision to take sanyasa, the disciples said that all women were not like Shamalambe, doing what their husbands wished them to. The Acharya's wife did not understand him, nor did she have any desire to. If he asked her to follow one path, she went along another, and upset him, they explained. So he left her to do whatever she wanted and decided to take sanyasa and devote his life to dharma.

Vadaganambi and his wife already considered the guru a great man, but after they heard this, their affection and respect for him increased. It is difficult to measure the extent of their devotion.

One afternoon, nearly two years after they had started looking after him, the Acharya was bathing in the pond. On one side of it there was a peepal tree. As he stood up after a dip, chanting some mantras, he glanced towards the tree. He felt that there was a woman peeping at him from behind it. As soon as his eyes turned in her direction, she hid herself. He wondered why any woman would behave in such a strange manner. He had not been able to see the face clearly. Perhaps it was someone who had come to the pond, either to wash her clothes or carry water from it, and was waiting for him to finish his bath, he thought. She must be someone from outside the village. The people of Saligrama had no such inhibition about the Achmya, as they knew his routine. The Acharya finished his bath and went into the temple.

That night, while talking to the guru about the day's happenings in the village, his disciple told him that a lady from the south had come there with an old companion. When they had asked who she was, she had told them that her husband had a problem and she had undertaken a pilgrimage to the north, hoping to find a cure for it. Her companion had taken ill, so the lady had requested Shamalambe to let them stay with her for a couple of days. Shamalambe had agreed. She made place for them in one part of the house and gave them all that they needed. The Acharya listened to this as he usually did to all other matters. Then a discussion of vedanta followed.

The next day, the Acharya received news that both the disciples in Thondanuru were ill. A strange epidemic had spread across the country that year. The guru immediately went to see them. The day he returned from there, he too had a fever. Despite this, there was no change in his routine of three baths in the pond, a single meal at noon, and milk at night. This went on for three days. His body rebelled against it and the fever raged. The disciple and his wife stayed by his bedside throughout and attended to his needs.

The worst thing about the fever was the severe pain in his body. When the guru sat up, leaning against the wall, and complained of the pain in his legs, Shamalambe quickly began to massage them. He pulled them back saying, "Don't, my child."

"Why? Is it wrong for your son-in-law and daughter to press your legs?" asked the disciple. "Let our lives become fulfilled by serving you," he added.

Thus, one of them, the disciple, Shamalambe or Ramachandra, was constantly beside him, to press his legs.

There was no change in his condition the next day and the pain in his body was as intense as before. Shamalambe spent all her time in the temple except when she went home to prepare food. Her husband went out only when he had to boil the milk or have his bath and his meal. The rest of the time he spent praying for his guru's recovery. During the day, Ramachandra and Shamalambe took turns to massage the Acharya's legs, but the boy could not do it at night. He was young and would fall asleep. So Shamalambe divided her night between sitting close to the guru and keeping vigil, or resting in the yard behind the sanctum sanctorum ...

It was midnight. Shamalambe, lying down a little distance away from the Acharya's bed, had just dozed off. She woke up with a start when she heard the Acharya call, "Who's that?" She quickly went to his side. Though her gaze was fixed on him, in the dim light of the lamp, she thought she saw someone walking away from his bedside. By the time she made the flame bigger and looked, there was no one there. She was a little frightened, but she could not brood on it. She was anxious to make sure the guru was all right. "What is it, Appaji?" she asked. "It's you, is it?" he said. "Yes," she replied. The Acharya fell silent.

She took the lamp and went outside the temple but found nobody there. She spoke to her husband about the incident. "Why did you lie down so far away? You should have been by his bedside," he scolded. "Who could have come so close to his bed? I'm frightened," said Shamalambe.

"Who would dare to go to his bedside here, in the temple of Narasimha? Must be a god or a devi or an alwar, come to look after our guru. There are many who will take care of him even if we don't." Shamalambe did not mind that her husband had scolded her. In fact, she was reassured to know that it was not anything to be afraid of. At that moment, she had thought it was the evil spirit of the fever which had come there to make the guru's condition worse. And she had seen it walk away. Because of her great affection for her guru, it had not occurred to her that such a thing was impossible in that holy place. Her husband's words had made her realise this, and satisfied, she returned to the Acharya's bedside.

By the grace of God, the guru's temperature came down the next morning and he even accepted some food that was given to him. The disciple and his wife were relieved. Shamalambe did not say so to her husband, but she was sure that it was the spirit of the fever she had seen the previous night.

Though the Acharyaimproved, the task of nursing the sick continued for Shamalambe. When she went home, she found that the lady from the south had taken ill. Shamalambe gave her a kashaya of medicinal herbs, provided her with all that she needed for her meal, then went back to the temple. The guru was telling Vadaganambi about a dream he had had the previous night ... He was in bed with fever. There was a severe pain in his legs. He was aware that Shamalambe had come to his bedside a number of times to press them. Some time during the night, he had dozed off. That is when he felt someone else come near him and massage his leg. It was a very different touch. Shamalambe's hands were those of a daughter. These were the hands of a married woman. He had felt his breath catch in his throat. He woke up with a start and asked who it was. He knew that someone was walking away from his bedside just as Shamalambe was coming towards him ... While the guru spoke of his dream, the disciple recalled what his wife had told him that night. Shamalambe confirmed what the guru had said, but held back her impression that someone had walked away even as she came in. Or that the spirit of the fever must have done something with his leg as it left. How could she talk about such a typically feminine intuition to either her husband, or the guru?

For a while, the disciple sat there wondering what the Significance of the guru's experience was. But what was the use of continuing a discussion about something which eluded his grasp? Besides, the Acharya was still not well enough. The matter could wait for a few days.

By some miracle, the guru went back to his routine the very next day. It became possible for both the disciple and Shamalambe to pay a little more attention to their own work. A couple of days later, the disciple told the Acharya that the condition of the lady from the south had worsened. Shamalambe had said the same thing when she sought permission to go back home earlier than usual. The next day, the disciple was late. He explained to the Acharya that the lady had died that morning. Before she died, she had requested Shamalambe to ask her husband to perform the obsequies for her. He had agreed because he believed that it was his duty as a brahmin to do it. That is why he was late.

"She came from some distant place and passed away here," said the Acharya, a little sadly, and then went back to his daily worship.

Shamalambe came to the guru in the evening. She did a namaskara to him and to her husband, and sat down. It was obvious that she had been crying. For a long time she did not say a word. After a while, the Acharya himself spoke. "Look, child, one shouldn't mourn excessively even on the death of a near one. She came to you seeking shelter. You took care of her. She passed away. Your husband performed the last rites as if he was her son. So why do you grieve?"

Shamalambe tried to say something, but the intensity of her grief choked her. No words came out only sobs. She fell at the Acharya's feet, weeping bitterly. After a few moments she did say something, but her words were so indistinct that he could not understand anything. The guru consoled her and told the disciple, "She is very distressed. Take her home."

The disciple came the next morning. From his appearance, it was apparent that he, too, had been crying. "Should you be grieving so much?" the Acharya asked him. The disciple controlled his grief and said, "Your daughter will tell you everything today."

When Shamalambe came that evening, she was calm and there were no signs of anguish on her face. She touched the guru's feet and sat down beside him. Her husband asked her to speak. She looked at the Acharya for a moment, then said, "I don't know how to begin ..." After a pause, she continued, "I thought the lady who died yesterday was a stranger. I found out before she died that she was, in fact, very close to all of us."

The Acharya sat there silently, listening to her.

"That is why I agreed that my husband would perform the last rites for her. She whispered to me about your relationship with her. She was our Acharya's wife before he renounced the world."

There was no change in the expression on the Acharya's face. All he said was, Narayana.

After a moment, Shamalambe spoke. "She told me that there was something for which she wanted to seek his pardon. I promised to speak to you about it. You must forgive her."

"It is only till the moment before one attains God's feet that all relationships, courtesies and pardons – in short, the dharma of this world – are valid. There is nothing for me to forgive in a life that has already reached His presence."

"I must tell you something on her behalf. She thought that there would be no salvation for her even in Heaven if you were to get angry on hearing it. If you say that you have forgiven her, I will tell you."

"Go on, child. I have forgiven her," the Acharya replied.

"It seems the Acharya's wife had behaved in this thoughtless manner because she had not understood his greatness. She was young and inexperienced. She knew nothing of life. Her husband was twenty-five years older than her. Besides, she came from a very orthodox family. Because of all this, her behaviour was so graceless. The Acharya was unhappy with her, and so she had to be a widow, even though her husband was alive. She was terribly distressed by the whole thing."

"It was God's will. No one was responsible for what happened.

Where's the question of forgiveness in this?"

"When she was at her mother's place, she heard you had come this way after you left the Chola land. She was very troubled about it. She reached here by asking people for directions to this place, with only one desire – to steal a Sight of you. She watched from her hideout, and made sure that the ascetic here was no one else but you. She intended to leave that day, but didn't. On the one hand was her companion's illness, on the other was the desire to see you once more. She extended her stay by a couple of days, but by that time you were taken ill. She didn't want to love before you improved. She got daily reports from us about your condition and suffered greatly when your fever raged and you were in pain. I didn't understand her concern then, but I do now."

"Forty years ago, I renounced all my bonds with the family. What's the message that's being conveyed to me today through all this?"

"This was a prelude to what I have to say now."

"When you were so ill, your wife prayed to God asking Him to spare you and give your illness to her. You remember that night when your fever was really high? I had stayed here for a while and then gone away to rest in the yard. She came to your bedside in my absence and by touching your leg, drew your fever to herself."

"What?" the Acharya exclaimed.

"As she touched your feet, she was overwhelmed by memories of the day she married you and couldn't help massaging your leg. That was when you woke up and asked, Who is that? And I came in. She took to her bed the very next day. She wanted me to ask you to forgive her for having desecrated your body with her touch, a body over which she had lost her claim long ago, and thus lowered the quality of your tapas."

The Acharya did not say anything.

Shamalambe continued, "The Acharya's wife gave us these three things along with her blessings," and showed him the jewels. After a while, the guru said, "The path of every life is pre-ordained. Each one takes its own course to reach the destination. Mine had to be this. May yours be happy."

Ramachandra was playing outside. The Acharya called him in and said, "Annayya, let's have the stotra: Lakshminarasimha mamadehi karavalambam." The boy's rendering of the stotra was sweet and they all enjoyed listening to him.

The companion of the Acharya's wife came to the Acharya the next day, took his blessings and left for her hometown.

I was slightly depressed as the story unfolded itself in my mind. I looked around to see where I was. I was under the peepal tree beside the pond. My gaze rested on the temple, the pond, the village. The light from the setting sun was a protective cover over the history of many centuries, like the wings of a bird sitting on its eggs to hatch them, like the waves of an ocean engulfing a million lives within it. My mind was in the grip of a wordless pain and a wordless yearning. An ascetic and his wife ... a disciple, his wife and their son ...

Trying to visualise all of them, I walked away from that place.

An Unfortunate Woman

A police officer I know told me this story.

Forty years ago, I was the prosecuting Inspector in one of the courts of the city. One day, an Inspector from another division had brought a young man, charged with murder, for trial. My job was to examine the witnesses and provide the magistrate with relevant details. It was then that I came across this tragic tale.

She was a young girl. She was pretty. Came from a small village on the road between Kunigalu and Hebburu. The name of the village was ... I cannot remember it. Her parents had five daughters and she was the first-born. The family was poor. The girls had to be married. But how? The father was worried. One day a young man from a neighbouring village came to him and said, "I have decided to take up a job in Bangalore and settle there. I don't want to go alone. I want to get married. Give your first daughter in marriage to me and I'll take her with me to Bangalore." This was an unexpected good fortune. The boy was tall and handsome. The father made a few enquiries about the antecedents of the boy, then gave his consent. The marriage took place. The couple left for Bangalore soon after.

They rented a place very near the market in the city. It was a small house with three rooms in it. The girl was not very knowledgeable about these things, but she knew what a man-woman relationship involved. Neither during the two days they spent in the village after the wedding, nor in the first few days in Bangalore, did the boy make any advances to her. They were still strangers to each other. She wondered why, but did not worry about it. Let her come to know me a little, let her get over her inhibitions – he must be thinking, she told herself. And she waited.

Three days later, the young man told her that he had found some work and that he would get paid about three or four rupees a day. He had bought some provisions with the few rupees he had brought from the village and she had cooked for him. Now that he had a job, he bought more things for the house.

A week passed. One evening, he brought a man with him. "This is a friend of mine. Make some tea for us," he told the girl. She had not even seen tea while she was in the village. On the day they arrived in Bangalore, they had gone to a tea-shop and had some.

While they were sitting there, he had told her how to make tea. He also showed her how to prepare some phalahara. Soon she had started making them at home. She gave the guest and her husband some of the snacks and the tea. After chatting with the guest for a while, her husband told her, "I have to go to the market. My friend will stay here. Don't be scared. He will look after you." He went out and pulled the door shut behind him.

Her heart started pounding. She could not make head or tail of her husband's words. To bring a stranger home, to leave her alone with him, saying that he would look after her, and that there was no need to be scared ... What did it mean? He had also shut the door behind him. She did not know all the facts yet her thoughts raced and she realised that something was wrong.

What should she do? How should she conduct herself?

A moment later the guest said, "Come, girl. Sit here, beside me. My friend has asked me to look after you," and gestured to a place by his side.

There was puzzlement in her eyes. "I don't know what my husband has said to you. I cannot even make any sense of what he told me. Don't try to act familiar with me. Go now. I'll talk to my husband when he returns and find out what he expects me to do."

"You infant! Your husband brought me here, told you to make tea for me, left the two of us alone, saying that I would look after you and that you don't need to be scared. Can't you guess why he did that? Are you really so innocent, you don't know how to bite the finger that is put in your mouth?"

So saying, the man took out a packet from the inside pocket of his coat. He opened it and held out a garland, a bottle of perfume and some milk pedas. "All these are for you. Take them. Sit next to me. I came here to be with you. That's why your husband brought me here."

The girl believed him. What was the game her husband was playing? He did not stay himself, instead he brought someone else. Did he get married for this?

After a moment or two, .she said, "Let me ask my husband first. Not now. Come some other time."

The man realised that she was indeed an innocent girl.

Though his ways were not what society would approve of, he was certainly not evil. He did not force himself on her. "All right then. I'll go," he said, opened the door and walked out.

The husband came home a couple of hours later. His wife was in an inner room. In the middle one, the garland, the packet of pedas and the bottle of perfume, all lay on the floor. The guest had gone. "Where is he?" the husband asked his wife.

"How do I know where he is? He said that he was my husband, not you. I sent him off saying that I would find out from you first and he could come back some other time."

"Ayyo, you silly girl! What happiness can I give you as your husband? The most I can earn in one day is three or four rupees. He gave me ten rupees even before he came here. See" He took a ten rupee note which was tucked in his waist band, and continued, "Keep it. It's yours. Eat whatever you want and buy whatever clothes you like. Live like a real queen. Look after me. I'm just a coolie and you are my wife. Our life is no life. This is life. Lots of money and happiness."

The girl was taken aback by his words. What she knew was that no husband would tolerate his wife looking at another man. But this one, he was so different ...

What was wrong with him? He had not behaved like a man with her. It could not be mere inhibition on his part. Was he not a man? Why had he become like this?

How could she find out the truth? He himself had done nothing. Instead he had brought a strange man home. She could only make a guess.

He was no man.

"I want to ask you something. Will you tell me the truth?" "What do you want to know?"

"We have been married for a week. You haven't touched me even once. Why? Aren't you a man?"

"No."

She had guessed as much but she still felt deeply hurt when she learned the truth. She felt pain and despair for a moment. But then she said, "Did you marry me so that you could make a living by selling me to other men?"

"Yes."

"Aren't you ashamed?"

"No."

"Do you realise that you have destroyed me?"

"I haven't done anything like that. You won't lack anything. I'll fetch royalty to your door. You will reign over them. What kind of comfort will you have if you are my wife?"

The girl was utterly disgusted by the attitude of her man who was no man. But the very next moment, she felt a great pity for him.

Poor fellow! He had a woman he could call his own, but could not live with her. What sort of a life was this for the unfortunate creature!

She spoke after a pause. "I cannot imagine doing what you have suggested. Let the night pass. I shall give my answer later."

She thought all night. What he was suggesting was indecent.. Suppose she said No. What could she do? Go back to her village? Say that he was not a man and that the marriage was no marriage? She would have to stay with her parents and be an object of ridicule. How thrilled she had been when he had come to ask for her in marriage! She would have danced with joy, but for the fear that others would make fun of her. There is no greater boon for a girl who has come of age than a suitable boy who offers to marry her. How happy her parents were. She was a lucky one, they thought! It was the same with all the other relatives. They had no reason not to believe that she was going to Bangalore to live with her husband. She had been so excited ... The shame that would be hers if she went home because of a marriage that was not a real marriage, would equal the thrill she experienced when she got married. Fate was asking her to choose between a life of shame at home, and this existence thrust on her by her husband.

She could not sleep till midnight. Then she dozed off only to wake up soon after. Her mind seemed to have cleared. In that state, she decided to stay with her husband and do what he wanted. That was the best thing under the circumstances.

She spoke to her husband in the morning. "I thought of going back home. My parents will be heartbroken if I do, and people in the village will make fun of me. I don't want that to happen. I accept the life you have offered."

The man who had come the previous day turned up that evening. She welcomed him and spent the night with him. He was not her husband but he wanted her. She was not averse to him. How nice it would have been if he had married her! But that was not to be.

She felt no disgust.

She told her husband the next day, "Don't bring a man home every day just for the sake of money. I'll tell you when I want one."

"All right. I won't. But remember that we won't have any money on those days."

"Doesn't matter."

"As you say."

Another thought occurred to her at lunch-lime. "Don't expect me to say yes to everyone you bring. If I don't like him, I will say I'm not well. You should send him back. You shouldn't force me against my will."

"I have already told you that I won't insist. But a man who has paid for your company will be furious if you turn him away. We shall have to return his money."

"I don't care. I can't have sex with a man I don't fancy."

"All right."

Everything was fine for the next ten days. One evening, her husband brought home a customer. She said she was not feeling well. He told the man, "She isn't well, it seems. Come a couple of days later." The man was furious. "You are an ass! Why did you accept money from me and bring me here before checking whether she was well or not?" and he used a filthy word.

Thrusting the money at him, the husband said, "Take your money and go. I don't want any trouble here."

The customer left. The husband went out to bring another one. It so happened that the first man was passing that way a little later, when he saw the husband talking to someone. A customer? Curious to find out, he stood in the shadow of the house opposite and watched ...

What's this? The husband and the man went to the house. The door opened. They went in together. Two seconds later, the husband came out, alone. He could hear the door being bolted from inside.

"When the door had opened to let the men in, the light had fallen on the customer's face. The man knew him. "She said she was not well to me, but has welcomed this one. That means she was rejecting me. The slut ... What arrogance"

He granted that this other man was young and good-looking, but ...

He had to teach them a lesson ...

The man was back at the same spot the next night, watching. The husband brought home a customer. The young man of the previous evening also turned up there at the same time. The three of them stood outside the house, talking softly among themselves. He could not hear what they were saying. After about five minutes, the door opened. The girl called the young man aside and said something to him. Then she told her husband, "I am not well. Tell your man to come another day." The husband handed back the money he had taken and sent him away. The young man too walked away in another direction. A little later, he returned and gently tapped on the door. It opened.

"I see, she doesn't want the man her husband had brought with him. She fancies this one," thought the man who was watching all this. Then he went away.

What was happening inside the house?

The girl really liked the young man. She unburdened herself to him.

"You aren't married, are you?"

"No."

"Are you satisfied with this arrangement, with these occasional visits? Do you feel you want to share your life with me?"

"What's the point of talking about it? You have a husband, remember."

"Would he have brought you here if he were a husband to me?

Or the ten others? True, he married me. But what did I get out of it? He is not a man. He lets me sleep with anyone who wants me and makes money from it. If you wish, you can give me a life. I like you. Do you like me?"

"Tell me what you want me to do, I'll do it."

"Talk to my husband and persuade him to give me up. I'll be your wife, your woman. I don't want you to have someone who is a leftover. Make the woman you desire your very own."

"All right. What you have suggested is fine. Let us see if he will agree."

"He may not, because it will mean a loss of income for him. But do anything. Make, him agree. Threaten him or bring pressure on him, if you have to. You are my only hope. Save me." So saying, she fell at his feet.

He picked her up. "It doesn't matter whether he is willing to let you go or not. I must fulfill the wishes of a girl who says she wants only me. I'll do it," he promised.

The next evening, the girl told her husband. "Don't bring anyone this evening. The man who came here yesterday is coming again. He wants to talk to you."

"He seems a good man," the husband said. "Not very generous with his money ... other customers offer two or three times more."

"Tell him that, then."

The young man was a little late. "I had left word saying that I wanted to talk to you. I take it you were waiting for me?" he asked the husband.

"Yes"

"You must not get angry at what I say. Listen carefully and do what I ask. There are three of us here. What I am going to suggest will be good for everyone."

"Go ahead."

"You are making money by handing over the woman you call your wife to a different man every day. This is not something a husband should do. It's certainly not an honourable thing."

"And so?"

"You are doing all this because you are impotent. Right?"

"Yes."

"You married this girl. But, it's not a marriage in the real sense, since you are not a man."

"No."

"Then let her go. I shall help you make your living some other way. It could be the end of what has been going on here."

"Leave her? Who do you think you are, to tell me all this? Don't stand here for a minute more. Get out."

"You important ass! Do you know what the people of this city will do to you if I tell them that you got married, so that you may live off your wife's earnings?"

"You are the ass here. You have the impertinence to come to

my house and say all these things to me? Shall I send for the police? They will kick you out of this place."

"You aren't the only one who knows the police, remember. What sort of a man are you? Being impotent, you told this girl's parents that you were a man. You deceived an innocent girl into marrying you and brought her here to live a dog's life. Now you threaten me saying that you are going to call the police. I'll tell them what business you are running. Do you know what they will do to you?"

"Get out. I'll have to kick you out if you don't leave"

"Go on then, kick me out, if you have the courage"

"Courage! You leave me no choice ..." The husband slapped the young man on the face. The girl, who was watching the heated argument between the two men and was apprehensive about how it would end, screamed, "You rascal, how dare you hit him!" She looked at the young man. His face was flushed with rage and humiliation. He pounced on the husband like a tiger and knocked him down. Covering his mouth with one hand, he hit him repeatedly on the head with the other. No sound came out of the husband as the young man squeezed his neck. He sat still for a moment without removing his hand, still squeezing his neck.

The husband was dead.

He stood beside the body, having finished off his beloved's enemy. The girl cried out, "What have you done? They will hang you for this."

"Let them. This son of a whore brought you to this state ... I was in a rage. But I didn't mean to kill him. It was my fury that did it."

"What do we do now?"

"Don't worry. No one knows what happened here. I will go and get a cart, take this body away and get rid of it somewhere. A body without a name and address, no one will know whose it is. You be brave. I'll go and get a cart."

"Ayyo, I can't stay here alone with the body. Take me outside. I will wait for you to return, and then join you."

"All right. Come."

He pulled her to him and reassured her. "Remember, I am your husband. We'll get married tomorrow. Don't worry about anything." He locked the house and they went out together. He took her home, and introduced her to his mother and his sister.

"I know this girl. She has come from another town and has to spend a night in the city. I told her that she could stay here and that you would look after her, Amma."

"All right appa," she said and welcomed the girl in.

The young man hired a jatka and went back to the girl's house. He somehow managed to stuff the body into a gunny-bag and tied it with a rope. He locked the house again, carried the sack to the cart and instructed the driver, "Take the road that leads to Banneraghatta."

The jatka started off.

All this while, the young man thought that there was no witness to these events. He did not know that the man who had been spumed by the girl earlier was looking for revenge, and was hiding in the shadow of the house in front, watching everything. The man did not know exactly what had happened, but was sure that something was wrong. There were three of them in the house that evening – the girl, her husband and the customer: The girl came out with the man. The husband? He might be inside, sleeping. But the lock? And the sack that he brought out? What was in it?

He desided to find out. The jatka has gone somewhere. The man would return in the same cart, he was sure. The cart would be parked in the jatka stand as usual. He would wait there for the owner of the horse and the cart.

We do not understand how far a man will go if he goes about it in such a single-minded way.

Just as he anticipated, the jatka returned to the stand after two hours. There were a couple of other jatkas with their drivers sleeping next to them. But the man went to the cart that had just come back and asked, "Coming? I have to go somewhere." The driver replied, "No ayya! My horse is very tired."

"What's your name?"

"Latif."

The man went home.

He returned to the girl's house the next morning. It was still locked. The girl had not come back. The young man must have taken her somewhere. To his own house? Perhaps. Where else could he take a girl who had fallen in love with him, in the middle of the night? He casually walked past the young man's house and saw her there.

It suddenly occurred to him that the young man must have killed the husband. The sack he had taken out of the house contained the body. He had transported it in the cart and buried it somewhere, he was sure. Good. He would inform the police and the two would get what they deserved.

He went to the police station, filled in all the details about the identity of the girl, the name and address of the man, and the name of the jatka driver who had carried the body. He told the police, "I have some suspicion. You can enquire into it."

And he went away.

Latif was found. He confessed that he had taken the body up to a certain spot on the road to Bannerghatta. The man who had hired the jatka had then carried the sack to a village nearby, he said.

The police used his cart to reach the spot. A crowd had assembled at the me entrance to the village. They told the police that they had found a gunny-bag at the bottom of the drain. There was a body in it.

No one in their village could recognise the man. Someone must have brought it from elsewhere and left it there.

The police from Bangalore had reached the spot just as the Patel of the village was setting out to report the matter to the nearest police station. The Inspector took charge of the body and brought it back to Bangalore.

There is not much to tell about what followed. The girl said in her statement, "This is the body of my impotent husband. That man is the one I love. He killed my husband in anger." The young man, in turn, told them what happened. "He was no man, that husband. He married her and brought her to Bangalore so he could sell her body and live off her. I told him to let her go, that he was doing something wrong. He wouldn't listen to me and used the foulest words possible about her and me. He slapped me and I was enraged. I knocked him down and strangled him ... I didn't mean to kill him, but that is what I did, anyway."

The Inspector recorded their statements very carefully and told him, "Homicide is a serious crime. What the husband did was immoral, utterly unethical. If you said that you were furious, and that you hit him in anger, without meaning to take his life, the court is sure to give you a lighter sentence. Are both of you prepared to make such a statement in the presence of the magistrate?" They said they would.

Both statements were recorded before a magistrate. I was the one who presented the case.

There was no problem questioning the witnesses. Everyone who listened to the cross-examinations agreed that the man, unfit to marry, had treated the girl with grave injustice. In the face of his crime, this act, of taking the life of a sinner, was not a crime. But neither I nor the magistrate could say such a thing, even if we felt that way. The magistrate ordered a trial before the Sessions Judge.

It turned out just as we thought. The defence lawyer argued, "This is not homicide. It is a case of causing death with no malice aforethought. I'm sure Your Honour will take the circumstances into account, and decide that justice, in this case, will be met by giving the lightest of sentences. I know I don't have to mention it ..."

I do not remember the details of the sentence given. I am certain it was not what is normally given in a case of homicide. May be a year or two of imprisonment.

Did he marry the girl after he came out? I do not know.

A Tale Told by Gouthami

When she visited her foster-father's ashram a with her son Bharatha, Queen Shakuntala spent the entire first night talking with her friends, Anasuye and Priyamvade. In the excitement of her visit., they had dropped all thoughts of their families, handed over the task of rocking the cradles to their husbands and chatted with her. Their grandmother,

Gouthami, bustled about with an alacrity which seemed impossible at her age, dividing her time between looking after them and attending to the affairs of the ashrama. When all the residents of the ashram a had retired for the night, she joined the girls in their conversation in the courtyard of the cottage.

Priyamvade teasingly remarked, "Look at ajji Gouthami, Shakuntala. Your arrival was enough to make her do a whole month's running about in a single day. An old woman till yesterday, she has turned into a young girl on seeing you."

"Who will say that Ajji is old? She is more active than any of us most of the time. But today, there is extra excitement in her," Anasuye said.

The old lady laughed. "You two are very clever. Don't I know you' With your flattering words, you will leave me to do all your work, so that you can spend time in the company of your queen. I have to turn into a girl if everything is to get done."

Priyamvade remarked, "So, Anasuye, we have discovered a cure for old age, haven't we?"

"May be, but it's not what you think," the old lady said.

The conversation came round to how Gouthami had brought pressure on Anasuye and Priyamvade to get married. Why had she been so insistent? Was she afraid that they too would be indiscreet, like Shakuntala had been with Dushyantha? Shakuntala was the daughter of an apsara. She had grown up expecting to marry a king. ButAnasuye and Priyamvade were girls from an ascetic background. They had not thought of marriage and family, so there was no reason to fear that they would succumb to temptation like Shakuntala had.

They talked about all this and more. Finally, the ascetic Gouthami said, "You do not understand these things. Even very young brahmacharis may go through what Shakuntala felt. Let me tell you about the experience of a girl I knew when I was young. Then I'm sure you will agree that I was fully justified in being anxious about you."

The three friends listened with rapt attention, as the old lady began ...

This young girl was one of the many children in the ashrama. She came from a village beyond the forest, and grew up here like all of you did. Children who are a burden to their father, because their mother is dead, those who are rejected by the family after the death of their father, those sent away in the name of service to dharma and those who hope for a better life than that in their own homes, come here. She too was one such child. Her name was Malini, the same name as our river.

Malini was about eight years old when she arrived. There were no girls of her age in the ashrama at that time. They were either four or five years younger or older. As a result, from the time she arrived at the ashram a, she moved about with the boys. She picked flowers, gathered leaves, looked after the cattle and took care of the visitors, just like any boy.

Among the children in the ashrama, two boys were her constant companions. Both were a little older than her. One was of Bharadwaja descent and the other had been adopted by the Kashyapas. Bharadwaja was about sixteen or seventeen and the other boy, Datta, was younger by a year or so. The girl had grown up with them and the thought that she was a girl never entered her head. The two boys also thought of her as a boy and related to her in a simple, natural manner, showing no reserve in dealing with her even after she grew up.

This was not unusual in Kanva's ashrama. The elders did not want boys and girls to grow up thinking that they were two entirely different species. We had all grown up in such an atmosphere. No wonder the girl and the two boys had no inhibitions in their relationship.

Because she was always with the two boys, Malini became an expert swimmer. Bharadwaja was, without doubt, the best swimmer in the ashrama, and Kashyapa was almost his equal. The world would not have seen another swimmer like Malini among the women.

One day, someone in the ashram a asked her in fun, which of the two boys she would have for a husband. Malini had never thought of marriage to either of them. But the next time she was with them, she found herself thinking about it. Her heart said Bharadwaja. It was not that she did not like Kashyapa. Both were equally dear to her. But, when it came to marrying, she settled on the older boy.

Meanwhile, the maharishi who was the head of the ashrama – our present head, Kanva, succeeded him later – sent for Bharadwaja and said, "Kashyapa and you have been very close to the girl, Malini. She has grown up. I would like to suggest you marry her." Bharadwaja did not say No, but walked away. Later, when Malini came near him, he found himself looking at her in a puzzled manner. A person he had taken to be a boy like himself must have, for the first time, appeared to him as a woman. He must also have thought of being discreet with her. He did not say a thing.

Malini, too, was as before with both of them, though she found herself drawn more and more towards Bharadwaja. He felt the same. One day, while the two of them were swimming in the river, he asked her, "Would you like to marry me?" The girl nodded her head. When they got out of the water, they told Kashyapa. His face looked as if a cloud had flitted across it. Kashyapa passed on the news to the inmates of the ashrama. The maharishi said he was happy to hear it.

Despite their decision to get married, the relationship between Bhardwaja and Malini did not change. The only difference was that they occasionally went away without waiting for Kashyapa. Malini loved to walk in the moonlight and look at the trees. She would ask the boys to go with her. If Kashyapa was not keen, she would go with Bharadwaja. The world has two sets of garments, Malini used to say, one for the day and one for the night. She believed that the flowers on a creeper or on a tree glowed with a strange magic in the moonlight.

There is, indeed, something magical about moonlight. Those who are caught in it, know. And Malini had been caught. Kashyapa went with them a couple of times but then he declined. Walking with the girl, Bharadwaja too came under its spell. He would stand and stare at her. She looked so desirable. If, to her, moonlight was a dress the world put on at night, to him it was Malini's dress. He felt the spirit of his love stood before him, clad in moonlight.

Often on such nights, when the tide in the river was low, they would go to the mound of the swans, in the middle of it. They would sit there together and experience the ultimate of marital bliss, a bliss which transcends the physical self.

'They would be married very soon.

It was the rainy season once more. You have seen how the Malini swells with fresh water during that time. Every Shravana, swimming across the river when it was in full flood, was a feat Bharadwaja had to perform. Datta, knowing his friend's mind, would join him. That year, when Bharadwaja talked about it, the girl felt like saying Don't, without knowing why. Bharadwaja laughed her fears away saying, "Without becoming a wife, you have already developed a wife's fears. I haven't become an old man since the last time I swam across the river!"

It was the night before the full moon. The sky was overcast. When the clouds lifted for a brief while, the two of them went to the sahakara tree beside the river. They sat on a rock in the moonlight, and spent a long time talking. Bharadwaja, who had never touched Malini with desire, suddenly held her face in his hands and kissed her. It did something to her. Her reserve was swept away, like trees by a river in spate.

They did not make love, but they became man and wife that night.

The time for the swim was fixed at two hours after daybreak. Almost all the young people in the ashram a gathered by the riverside as Bharadwaja and Kashyapa prepared themselves for the event.

The fiver was in full flood when they jumped into the water. You must have noticed how still the water looks as it flows over the topmost step of the ghat. It gives the impression of being motionless, particularly in the middle. Only when you see the grass, twigs and other rubbish floating along, do you realise it is moving.

The two young men swam side by side till they reached midstream. Then each one had to negotiate the rock very quickly, otherwise the current would carry him too far off the course. Bharadwaja was slightly ahead at this point. He also reached the other bank first. Datta joined him soon after. They walked about on the bank for a while before they plunged into the river again. They had to keep Yogashaila, the rock which was in the dead centre of the river, to their right, as they swam back. If you look at it now, you would think it is on one side. That is because the river has changed its course since then.

Much effort was needed to skirt it from the left. Otherwise they had to come from below it. Bharadwaja must have been tired that morning as he negotiated therock. Justas they reached the spot, an uprooted tree floated down towards the swimmers. It seems that Datta saw the tree. He realised it would crash into his friend. He shouted a warning. The people on the bathing ghat also saw the danger, and called out to him. Bharadwaja probably heard them, but did not understand what they were saying. He saw, their raised hands pointing to something and looked in that direction. Everyone saw him turn his head. At that moment, the tree hit him. They saw him go under, trapped in the branches of the tree. He did not come up again ...

Gouthami stopped. She went out of the hut saying, "Who is that?"

"There's no one there, but Ajji thought she heard someone call," said Priyamvade. Anasuye looked at Shakuntala. She just nodded her head.

The old lady returned after a few minutes and took up the narration again ...

Nobody is sure about what happened. The tree had become entangled with the rock in the river and the young swimmer had been caught between them. Each minute seemed like a lifetime, as Datta swam towards his friend. Those on the shore had to walk a thousand steps before they could dive into the water and reach the rock. Some started out, others dissuaded them. "Nothing will happen to Bharadwaja. He isn't an ordinary man," they said. Finally, two of the onlookers jumped into the water and reached Yogashaila. Meanwhile, Datta had risked his own life three times, trying to drag his friend on to the rock. The two men who had jumped into the river, helped Datta bring the body to the ghat.

Bharadwaja was dead. His soul was in the sky above. All that was left for the ashrama was his lifeless body.

The maharshi was shattered by the accident. A young life had been snatched away prematurely. There was still so much for it to give and take. He arranged for the last rites to be performed and banned swimming in the river when it was full. That was the last of such sport.

The ban did not bring Bharadwaja back. There was no way of undoing the dreadful thing that had happened.

Malini was one of those who had shouted a warning when Bharadwaja seemed to be in danger. The previous night, as they sat together, he had reassured her saying, "My eyes will be on you when I am in the water. You cannot know how much strength I get just from my desire to be with you. Others will know that I deserve you once I conquer the river. So, first the river, then the woman, followed by life, and finally meditation."

These were the four goals he had in mind, but his life had to end even before he had achieved the first one! The river, Malini, had turned out to be a rival of the girl, Malini, and swallowed the youth.

That was the end of the boy, but the girl was still there. Nobody seemed to think about her. In their eyes, perhaps, there was no reason to be concerned. Extreme mourning was taboo in the ashranla even when a husband died. And these two were not even married. So there were not many to weep for her. Only a couple of the inmates offered their condolences and comforted her.

Malini felt that her life had ended. She and Bharadwaja could have been married four years ago. As man and wife they could have had a physical relationship. Instead, they had nurtured a pure love. Like the child, Bharata, who had caressed the fruit we gave him this evening and held it to his nose before biting into it, they were garnishing the meal of life with love before savouring it. It was as if they had been forced to give up eating because a lizard had fallen on to the plate.

We know nothing more about the boy. Is there life after death? One does not know. What we do know is what happens here. Malini had been left behind, bereft. She did not cry, afraid of what the others would say. As a matter of fact, she did not feel like crying. Her grief was too great to be washed away by tears.

It seemed as if the unfortunate girl had, in losing Bharadwaja, lost Datta too. The three of them had been inseparable when they were young. Datta had distanced himself a little from them once they had decided to get married. It could not have been any other way, though he cherished them as before. Now Bharadwaja had gone away, and so had Datta, though he was very much there. A brother who was a brother no more.

Malini was alone in every way. For a while, all her thoughts were of Bharadwaja. Her eyes repeatedly filled with images of the winsome combination of his broad chest, shining eyes and firm gait. She savoured the memories of their last meeting by reliving them over and over again. A man's voice is pleasing to a woman's ear. There is an added dimension to it when it has the import of love. She remembered the special appeal ill it when they met for the last time. They had sat close to each other and there was an indescribable happiness in the mere contact of the two bodies. Just the memory of it was enough to make her swell with pleasure. She could believe that

Bharadwaja got stronger when he looked at her and was convinced that his shining eyes were fixed on her as she stood on the bank. It is not just a figure of speech to say that love is deathless.

Yes, it is true. But the loss of that love was equally real.

Malini almost went mad wondering how it could turn into nothing. There was no place for such madness in an ashrama meant for meditation. Why, then, had it not prevented her from going insane? There was no easy answer to that question. Not only had the ashrama not prevented her madness, it seemed to have abetted it. The mound where swans broke into pairs to make love, she used to go there with her avowed husband. He was no more, but the shadows of a young man and his girl still lingered between two shining streams of water. Only shadows, with no substance.

What sort of a meaningless existence was hers? For what purpose?

One day, unable to bear her grief, she jumped into the river. It was not easy for her to drown since she knew how to swim. Datta, who was walking along the bank looking for flowers and leaves, saw a body being carried away by the current. He pulled her out and saved her life. When she asked him why he had not let her die, he answered that Fate did not want her to.

She had to get on with her life even though she had no wish to live.

Days, months and years passed. Three years later, her grief was no longer as intense as it had been. Her memories were alive but there was no turbulence. She had attained a kind of peace. She mixed with the residents in the ashram a and was like everyone else. 'There was a naturalness in the way she related to Datta.

Datta had gone deeper and deeper into meditation and the kulapati of the ashram a looked upon him with great fondness. The people treated him with respect, as if they knew that he would be the next guru.

It was springtime and our sahakara tree had burst into flower. The jasmine creeper that had climbed up the tree, sprouted new shoots. Malini found herself assailed by strange desires. She did not know what she wanted. One day she found herself longing to meet Datta though there was no reason to visit him. Why did she want to see him so urgently? She suppressed her desire and tried to turn her mind to other things. But her mind would not listen to her. By the time she understood the nature of her longing, it had become her master. She fought against it for a few days, only to be defeated in the end.

Bharadwaja was supposed to be her husband. But that did not happen. Why could she not marry Datta? She could. She must. It had to be that way. There was no escape from the inevitable.

Datta had saved her hie. Surely he would take care of that life? A few days later, she went to him when he was alone. He turned to her. "What is it, Akka?" he asked, surprised.

There was no trace of shyness when Malini begged him to take her as his wife. "Let us not talk about it, Akka," he said.

They exchanged many words on the matter. "Wouldn't you have married me if, at that time, our guru had ordered you instead of Bharadwaja?" she asked.

"I might have said Yes, like Anna did. I don't know. Why bring it up now? You became my sister-in-law and I have looked upon you as such ever since. I can't think of you as my wife now," he replied.

"All this talk of brother and sister-in-law is a creation of the imagination, isn't it?" she argued.

"Yes, pure imagination."

But that which was nothing more than imagination had become a deep reality in his life. How could he say it Was not there? Every time he looked at her, he would see Bharadwaja by her side. Bharadwaja was not a figment of his imagination! When he came to know that Bharadwaja was going to marry her, he realised Fate intended him to attain salvation by remaining a brahmachari. Fate had directed him away from a family. He had to submit to that command and he needed his sister-in-law's help to obey it.

"Of the two who could have married me, Fate took away one. Now isn't Fate telling me to many the other?"

"It's not easy to read Fate's decrees. It's easy to deceive ourselves into believing that what we desire is what Fate dictates. We should carefully consider what is right, and then accept it as our destiny."

"Tell me, what is Fate asking me to do now?"

'Just as it told me not to think of marriage, it asked you to give up all thoughts of a family the very day Bharadwaja-anna died. I thought you knew that."

"What about this longing then? Surely, it's what Fate has given me."

"Haven't you heard our guru say that desire is like a snake. We should be on our guard so that it doesn't steal into the anthill of our bodies."

"It's like putting a snake and a mouse into one basket and then giving a warning. Of what use is it?"

Datta had nothing to say to this.

At that point Malini stopped arguing and turned her mind towards renunciation.

One more year went by. It was springtime again. Once more, the kokila's song was heard in the forest, the jasmine blossomed on the sprouting sahakara tree and desire stirred in the young girl's heart.

Desire is as natural and inevitable as new shoots on a tree and blossoms on a creeper. It is in the nature of a living tree to sprout, a growing creeper to flower, and a young life to desire. When the whole world was in bloom, drawing deep breaths of hope and longing, there was an awakening of love in Malini's heart too.

Sometimes, people ask each other in wonder, "Why does this man desire that object?" At such moments they forget their relationships with their own desires. It is not that a man desires something, it is more a case of desire taking him by the hand and leading him to it. Does the flotsam on a flowing stream choose its course? Can it? Man is also helpless like it, caught in the currents of life. Only a very small number out of every thousand show signs of life like dogs, foxes and men. But even they are powerless in the face of life's currents. There was no one more full of life than Bharadwaja but he too was swallowed by the river. So when desire becomes a raging current, is any living being safe? It has no regard for men. Those that can face it are the ones in whom desire does not rage. It only picks out those who cannot withstand its onslaught. A strong tree manages to reach the other shore, but a helpless blade of grass is swept away by the flow. Like a powerful current, desire knocked Malini down that springtime, and carried her away without any pity.

Malini was determined to get Datta somehow. She went to him one day. "I have come to you seeking alms," she said.

Datta used many arguments to make her understand his position.

Finally he told her that it was impossible for him to think about marriage. What could Malini say? She swallowed her words and went away.

It was Vasanta Pournima the following day, celebrated as a festival in the ashrama. When the inmates retired for the night, Datta made his way to a sequestered spot and sat down to meditate.

Malini lay down in her hut but sleep would not come. I have mentioned her fondness for moonlight. She came out to take a walk. She wandered around the ashram a listlessly, and found herself at the spot where Datta had sat down for meditation. She had not planned to go there, but she had reached there unconsciously, involuntarily.

Datta had fallen asleep. His bare upper body was bathed in moonlight. There was the characteristic guileless and peaceful smile on his face. Malini seemed to believe that it was Bharadwaja, not Datta, who was sleeping there. She sat near his head, caressed his cheek with her right hand and ran her fingers over his chin affectionately.

Datta woke up and saw her. He sat up with a start and asked, "Why have you come at this hour, Akka? Couldn't you sleep?"

He could as well have asked why she was behaving in this insane manner! But Datta was a sober and considerate man, incapable of pointing accusatory fingers at the erring ways of others. Not only would he not say anything, he would not even think of it. His eyes refused to see a wrong if the person was repentant for having committed it.

"You are right. I couldn't sleep. I felt like coming to you, so here I am," Malini replied.

"Akka, I understand your feelings. How beautiful the moonlight is! I went to the river and sat down for a while, watching the water shimmer under it. The night is so peaceful," Datta said.

Malini was silent. After a pause she asked, "You have to tell me something."

"About what, Akka?"

"You know it."

"I've already given you my answer."

"What answer?"

"That I don't want to get married."

"It doesn't matter if we don't get married. Let us live together." Datta was not prepared for a statement like this from her. The core of conviction inside him must have trembled under its impact. He took a full minute to recover, then said, "What's to stop us ? We are together even now, aren't we?"

"Don't pretend you don't understand what I meant. I am not ashamed for you to know it. Would I have approached you like this if I felt any shame?"

"Tell me, Akka, is this an alternative to the path of brahmacharya that rejects marriage?"

"Set fire to this sister-brother relationship. You keep talking of something quite unrelated to what I'm saying. Look, life is becoming impossible for me. Take me once and let me have you once. Just once. Never again. If you say No, I'll drown myself."

"Didn't Fate prove to you last year that it wasn't the way out?"

"Was it Fate, or was it you? Why did you have to save her, who jumped into the river, wishing to end it all? To see her suffer like this? I would have lived in death. You saved me, only to kill me later."

"Akka, it's not in your hands to live, nor is it in my power to save. There's a force outside which looks after life, don't forget. You are a wise person. You are my sister-in-law, capable of showing me the way. Though younger in years, you are older in wisdom. So take me by the hand and lead me on the right path."

Malini stood still for a moment. Suddenly, she lunged at him with outstretched arms, wanting to grab his face and pull it towards her breasts.

Datta was equally fast in recoiling from her. He prostrated before her, holding her feet with both hands. "Protect me. Don't put me to the test," he pleaded. "You are a woman, Adishakti, the primeval force. There's nothing like a fall for you. I am a man. I can never hope to keep my soul pure. It's only with your blessings that I can succeed. If you are adamant, I will lose my way. Bless me, I beg you, and save me." There was complete surrender in his voice.

Malini's virtuousness came to her rescue at that moment. The helplessness in his plea sparked off a strange emotion in her heart. It tore the scales from her eyes without her realising it. Datta, the adult who could resist her, suddenly seemed to have changed into a helpless child who could survive only with her support. Her arms which had reached out to embrace him as a man now desired to hold him as an infant seeking comfort. She held him to her, ran her fingers through his curls, caressed his cheeks and stroked his back with tenderness. She raised his head, kissed his face and got up.

Datta too stood up.

"You are right. I must go," Malini said, and made her way to her hut.

With the blessings of the elders and the quality of Datta's tapas,

Malini was never again caught in the whirlpool of desire. As Datta grew in moral stature, the kulapati knew he had found his successor and looked upon him with pride. Malini, like a mother or a sister, was proud of his achievements and considered them her own. Datta became a noble soul and Malini was redeemed.

It was Datta's nobility that had saved Malini. What would have happened to her otherwise? What would have been her fate? And his? Due to Datta's unswerving faith, both of them were able to stay on the path of dharma and conquer unhappiness. Whenever I think of this, I feel that men with such strong principles, like Datta, are truly very rare. If it had been any other man, she would have been a sinner that night. She was glad she had gone looking for him and had been saved.

Malini's punya too must have been of a high order. What would have happened to a girl with less strength, caught in such a whirlpool of passion? That is why I insist that girls should get married when they are still young. Of course, not all girls are Malini. The desire to get married may not be there in all of them. They may not lose their way, even if they did have such a desire. Not everyone will wander about like she did, I know. But still, we should remember what youth can do. The case of one who grows up thinking of nothing but meditation, is different. A girl who wants to marry should get a mate at the right time. Shakuntale, do not feel bad at what I say, but it is because you did not get married at the right age, that you lost your heart as soon as you set eyes on the king. You two were on her side in the matter, Priyamvade and Anasuye! You considered me, who brought you up, an outsider and thought of the outsider as a kinsman. That is why, girls, I insisted at that time that I would not be at peace till you got married.

The ascetic came to the end of her story. The girls did not say anything for a while. It was Priyamvade who broke the silence. "Ajji, what you told us is like a story and most unlike history. You wouldn't have known all those details if it were just history, would you?"

Anasuye smiled as she turned towards Shakuntala. "What do you say, Shakuntala? If it is history, how does Ajji know all the details?"

Shakuntala nodded.

"What is it that the two of you know and I don't?" Priyamvade asked.

"I need Ajji's permission before I can tell you anything," Anasuye said.

"Go ahead, girl. There's no reason to hide anything," Goutharni said to her.

"Malini was none other than our ajji, Gouthami.". Gouthami confirmed it.

"How you must have suffered, Ajji! I tremble at the very thought of what you must have gone through. Where is Datta? What happened to that noble soul?" Priyamvade exclaimed.

"I can tell you that if Ajji allows me," Anasuye said.

"You know everything I know. Tell her, let her also know."

"Datta is the kulapati of our ashrama."

"I would have told you myself if you had waited a minute, believe me. You remember when Ajji went out? I guessed she had wiped her eyes when she returned. I thought her grief was for the suffering of her childhood friend. She was narrating the whole thing as if it had nothing to do with her. I was under the impression that it was someone else's story . The details were so personal but the narration so objective that I was fooled."

"If Datta wasn't what he was as a youth, would my father have been what he is now?" Shakuntala commented. "The head of the ashrama faced a desire which was like a river in spate, able to sweep away everything in its course. Bharadwaja was a noble youth, but certainly not the equal of Datta. One in a million may have the nobility of my father, not one in a thousand."

"Now I understand why our kulapati has so much respect for Ajji. She is younger in years but he treats her as an elder," said Anasuye.

"You are right, child. He has often said that it is easy for one to cross a stream with a thin trickle of water but not one which is in flood. He has spoken of me as one who has crossed a river in spate and reached the shore beyond. Not that he has had no desire, but it was never a river in full flow as it was in me, according to him. Who can measure desires? Our kulapati is an influential person and that is why our ashramais such a great place. We have a king for a son-in-law and our grandson will be an emperor."

"Your words are sweet, Ajji, as they describe the greatness of my father," said Shakuntala. "There is something else which is equally dear to me and that is your tender heart. It's because you knew such great suffering yourself that you are able to respond to ours. The deer of the ashram a becomes your child and the chakravaka your friend. How gentle you are!"

Gouthami got up. "Come on, girls. It's late and you must go to bed," she said. She stroked Shakuntala's cheek and patted the heads of Anasuye and Priyamvade. Then saying, "Don't stay up too long, girls. Go to sleep," she made her way to her hut.

MASTI VENKATESHA IYENGAR

1891 June 6: Masti Venkatesha Iyengar is born at Masti, in the Kolar district of Karnataka.

1907 Masti passes his matriculation examination from the Wesleyan High School, Mysore, with a first class first.

1909 He joins Maharaja's College, Mysore, for first year BA and obtains a first class. History is his favourite subject and his interest in it remains with him throughout his life.

1911 *Yedurayana Vijaya*, Masti's first short story, is published in a periodical, *Madhuravani.*

1912 Masti gets a first class first at the BA examination with Physics and Chemistry, from Central College, Bangalore.

He is married to Pankajamma.

1914 Masti is awarded a gold medal for standing first at the MA examination in English, from Madras University.

1917 Masti joins the Mysore Civil Service after getting the top rank in the competitive exam. He is appointed Assistant Commissioner, Excise.

1920 His first collection of short stories, *Kelave Sanna Kathegalu*, also the first collection of short stories in Kannada, is published by MVJK Trust, Bangalore. It includes "Ranga's Marriage," "An Old Tale" and "Our Teacher."

1922 Binnaha, a collection of his poems is published.

1925 An essay on the function of literary criticism, *Sahityadal li Vimarseya Karya*, is published.

1926-33 *Vimarse*, in four volumes, released.

1929 Masti presides over the annual Kannada Sahitya Sammelan at Belgaum. He is the youngest person ever to be given this honour.

1930 Masti is promoted as Deputy Commissioner.

1934 *Sanna Kathegalu 4* published. It contains "Venkatashami's Love Affair," "Jogyora Anjappa's Chicken" and "The Pandit's Will."

1935 *Rabindranatha Thakuraru*, a biography of Tagore in three volumes, edited by Masti, is released on the occasion of Tagore's birth centenary celebrations

1936 *Sanna Kathegalu 5*, which includes "Mangamma, the Curd-Seller," is published.

1940 *Sanna Kathegalu 6* released. "The Acharya's Wife" is in this volume of Masti's short stories.

1942 Masti receives the Rajaseva Prasaktha Award from the Maharaja of Mysore.

He is invited to preside over the All India Oriental Conference at Hyderabad.

1943 Masti resigns from the Mysore Civil Service after being in it for twenty-six years.

He is elected Vice President of the Kannada Sahitya Palishad.

1944 *Jeevana*, a monthly magazine, edited and published by Masti, is launched.

1946 The South Indian Languages Conference, held in Hyderabad, is presided over by Masti.

1947 *Sanna Kathegalu 7* released. "A Tale Told by Goutharni" features in it.

1949 "An Unfortunate Woman" is published as part of Sanna *Kathegalu 9.*

1954 Kamataka University, Dharwar confers an honorary D Litton Masti.

1964 Masti accepts the vice-presidentship of PEN.

1968-69 Bhava, an autobiography in three volumes, is published. There is no reference to his literary career in it.

1969 Masti's wife, Pankajamma, passes away.

1969 *Sanna Kathegalu 12, 13* receive the Sahitya Akademi Award.

1972 Masti writes *Sahityada Preranegalu* as a post-script to Bhava It deals mainly with his literary activities.

1974 Masti is made a Fellow of the Sahitya Akademi.

1977 The University of Mysore honours Masti with a D Litt.

1983 Masti receives the Jnanpith Award for Chikaveera Rajendra, and for his contribution to Kannada literature.

1986 June 6: the end of an era – Masti passes away in the early hours of the morning.

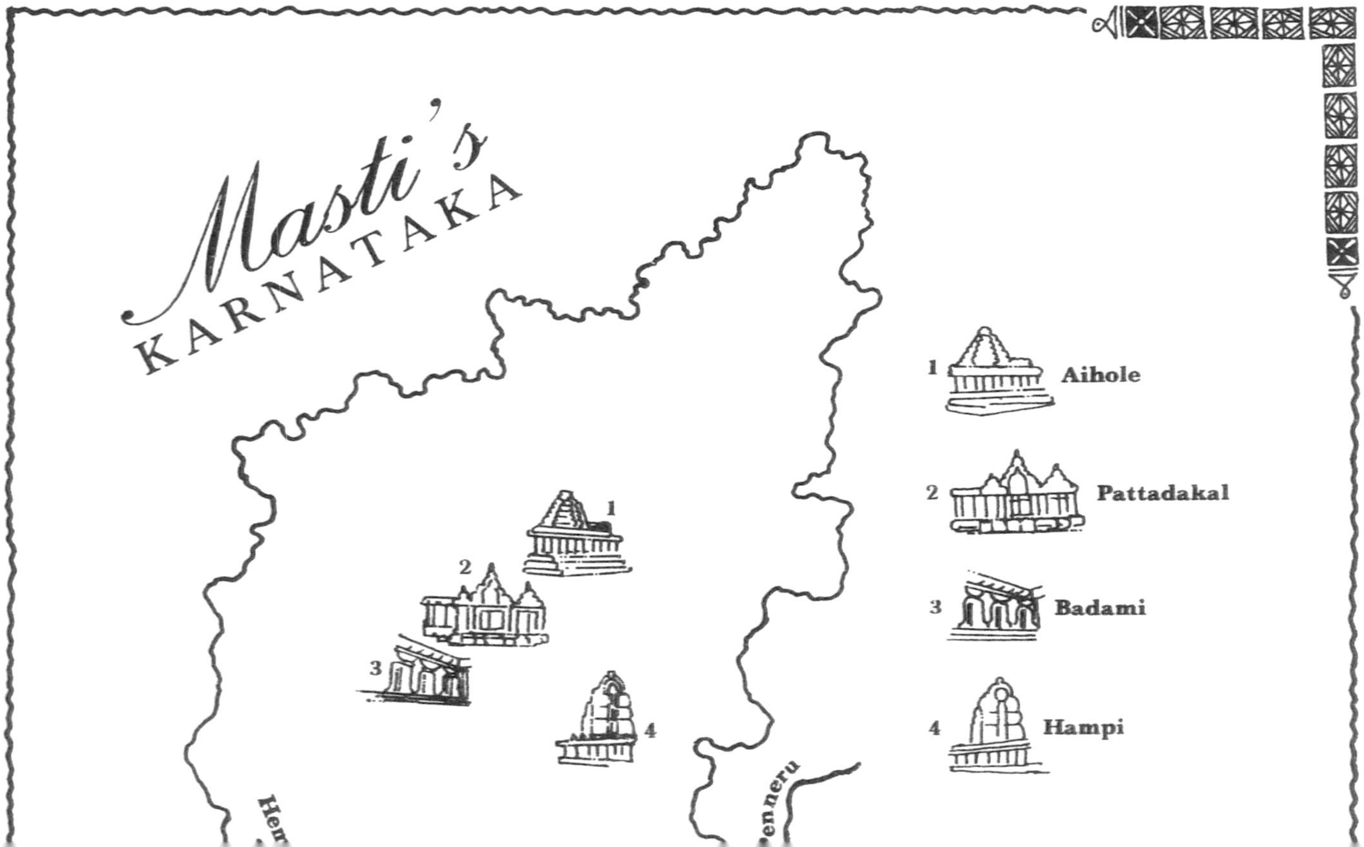
Masti's
KARNATAKA
1
2
3
4
1 Aihole
2 Pattadakal
3 Badami
4 Hampi

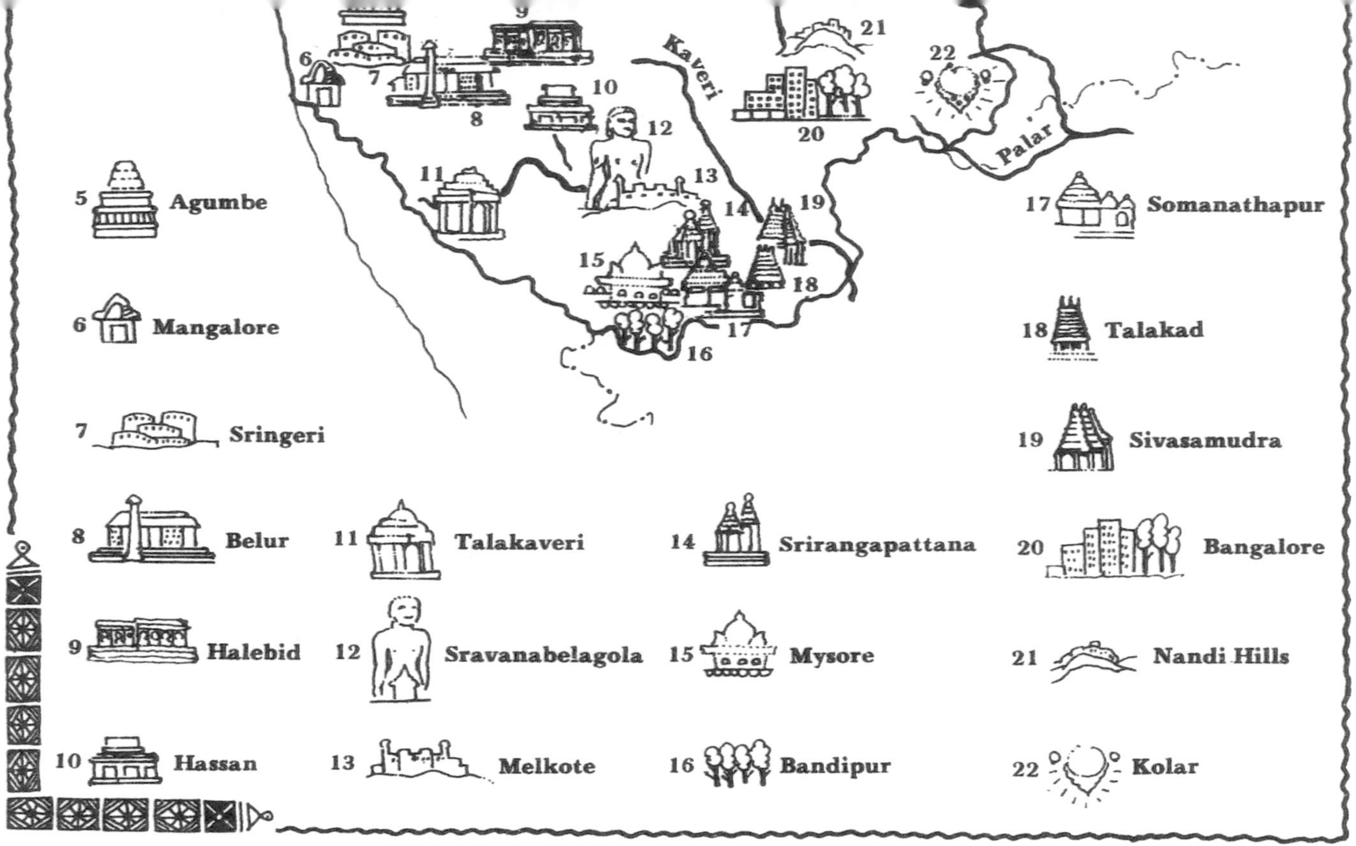
Kaveri
Palar
5 Agumbe
6 Mangalore
7 Sringeri
8 Belur
9 Halebid
10 Hassan
11 Talakaveri
12 Sravanabelagola
13 Melkote
14 Srirangapattana
15 Mysore
16 Bandipur
17 Somanathapur
18 Talakad
19 Sivasamudra
20 Bangalore
21 Nandi Hills
22 Kolar

BIBLIOGRAPHY

Works of Masti Venkatesha Iyengar

In Kannada

1.	*Kelavu Sanna Kathegalu*	(Some short stories)	1920
2.	*Binnaha*	(poetry)	1922
3.	*Shantha*	(Drama)	1923
4.	*Savitri*	(Drama)	1924
5.	*Sanna Kathegalu*	(Short stories – 2)	1924
6.	*Sahitya*	(Essay)	1924
7.	*Aruna*	(poetry)	1924
8.	*Vimarshe*	(Criticism)	1924
9.	*Usha*	(Drama)	1927
10.	*Subbanna*	(Novella)	1928
11.	*Talikate*	(Drama)	1928
12.	*Vimarshe – 2*	(Criticism)	1929
13.	*Nalku Sanna Kathegalu*	(Short stories – 3)	1930
14.	*Kannada Seva*	(Essay)	1930
15.	*Manjula*	(Drama)	1930
16.	*Tavare*	(Poetry)	1930
17.	*Janateya Samskriti*	(Essay)	1931
18.	*Cheluvu*	(poetry)	1931
19.	*Shivachatrapathi*	(poetry)	1932
20.	*Vimarshe – 3*	(Criticism)	1933
21.	*Yashadhara*	(Drama)	1933
22.	*Malara*	(poetry)	1933
23.	*Sanna Kathegalu*	(Short stories – 4)	1934
24.	*Ravindranath Tagare*	(Biography)	1935
25.	*Sanna Kathegalu*	(Short stories – 5)	1936
26.	*Shri Ramakrishna*	(Biography)	1936
27.	*Tirupani*	(Drama)	1937

28.	*Janapada Sahitya*	(Essay)	1937
29.	*Kakanakote*	(Drama)	1938
30.	*Adikavi Valmiki*	(Criticism)	1938
31.	*Vimarshe – 4*	(Criticism)	1939
32.	*Sanna Kathegalu*	(Short stories – 6)	1940
33.	*Gowdara Malli*	(Poetry)	1940
34.	*Ramanavami*	(Poetry)	1941
35.	*Mookana Makkalu*	(Poetry)	1943
36.	*Tainudiya Tammadi*	(Speech given as the president of the Oriental Conference)	1944
37.	*Navaratri – 2*	(poetry)	1944
38.	*Navaratri – 5*	(Poetry)	1945
39.	*Chitrangada*	(Translation of Rabindranath Tagore's play)	1945
40.	*Navaratri – 3*	(Poetry)	1946
41.	*Suneetha*	(Poetry)	1946
42.	*Prasanga*	(Articles)	1946
43.	*Sanna Kathegalu*	(Short stories – 7)	1947
44.	*Sanna Kathegalu*	(Short stories – 8)	1948
45.	*Navaratri – 4*	(Poetry)	1948
46.	*Sanna Kathegalu*	(Short stories – 9)	1949
47.	*Chennabasavanayaka*	(Novel)	1950
48.	*Sanna Kathegalu*	(Short stories – 10)	1950
49.	*Manavi*	(Poetry)	1951
50.	*Poojana*	(Prefaces)	1951
51.	*Chintana*	(Essay)	1952
52.	*Bharata Teertha*	(Criticism)	1952
53.	*Navaratri – 1*	(poetry)	1953
54.	*Masti*	(Drama)	1953
55.	*Anarkali*	(Drama)	1955
56.	*Chikaveera Rajendra*	(Novel)	1956

57.	*Kannadalenka*	(Speech given at the convocation of the Karnataka University)	1957
58.	*Sanna Kathegalu*	(Short stories – 11)	1957
59.	*Hamlet*	(Translation of Shakespeare's Hamlet)	1958
60.	*Chandramaruta*	(Translation of Shakespeare's Tempest)	1959
61.	*Lear Maharaja*	(Translation of Shakespeare's King Lear)	1959
62.	*Dvadasha Ratri*	(Translation of Shakespeare's Twelfth Night)	1959
63.	*Shrikrishna Karnamrita*	(Translation from Sanskrit)	1959
64.	*Namma Nudi*	(Articles)	1960
65.	*Sir M. Vishweshwariah*	(Articles – Edited)	1960
66.	*Shakespeare Drishyagalu – 1*	(Scenes from Shakespeare – 1)	1964
67.	*Prasanga – 2*	(Essay)	1963
68.	*Purandaradasa*	(Drama)	1964
69.	*Shakespeare Drishyagalu – 2*	(Scenes from Shakespeare – 2)	1964
70.	*Shakespeare Drishyagalu – 3*	(Scenes from Shakespeare – 3)	1964
71.	*Prasanga – 3*	(Essay)	1965
72.	*Kanakanna*	(Drama)	1965
73.	*Sanna Kathegalu*	(Short stories)	1965
74.	*Sampadakeeya*	(Four collections of editorials in Jeevana)	1967

75.	*Sahitya Lalane*	(Letters)	1967
76.	*Prasanga – 4*	(Essay)	1967
77.	*Sanna Kathegalu*	(Short stories –12)	1968
78.	*Bhava*	(Autobiography in 3 parts)	1968-69
79.	*Bhattara Magalu*	(Opera)	1969
80.	*Sankranti*	(Poetry)	1969
81.	*Vichara*	(Articles)	1971
82.	*Shri Rama Pattabhisheka*	(Poetry)	1972
83.	*Banuli Drishyagalu*	(Radio plays)	1974
84.	*Sahitya Prerane*	(Speech)	1975
85.	*Sheshamma*	(Novel)	1976
86.	*Navaratna Ramarao*	(Speech)	1976
87.	*Patragalu*	(Letters)	1977
88.	*Kalidasa*	(Drama)	1978
89.	*Arambhada Angla Sahitya*	(Speech)	1979
90.	*Namma Hosa Sahityada Arambha*	(Speech)	1979
91.	*Archana*	(Speech)	1979
92.	*Prasanga – 5*	(Essay)	1980
93.	*Samkshipta Valmiki Ramayana*	(Ramayana – Abridged)	1981
94.	*Uttara Kanda Vichara*	(Essay)	1981
95.	*Antaragange*	(Essays)	1982
96.	*Ajjana Dari*	(Drama)	1983
97.	*Dharma Samrakshane*	(Essay)	1983
98.	*Sanna Kathegalu – 15*	(Short stories)	1984
99:	*Vimala Marianne*	(Drama)	1985
100.	*Matugara Ramanna*	(A narrative)	1985
101.	*Kathegalu – 1*	(Collected short stories)	1987
102.	*Kathegalu – 2*	(Collected short stories)	1988

Masti's Works in English

1.	*Popular Culture of Karnataka*	1937
2.	*The Poetry of Valmiki*	1940
3.	*Subbanna*	1943
4.	*Short Stories – 1*	1943
5.	*Short Stories – 2*	1943
6.	*Short Stories – 3*	1944
7.	*Short Stories – 4*	1944
8.	*Ravindranath Tagore*	1946
9.	*Short Stories – 5*	1968
10.	*Essays, Addresses*	1975
11.	*Rajaji – Volumes 1 and 2*	1975
12.	*Srimad Bhagavadgite: A Study*	1978
13.	*Kalidasa*	1980
14.	*Thoughts on Religion*	1983
15.	*Thinking of My Life*	1983

Masti's Novels in English Translation

1. *Subbanna*, 1943, translated by the Author, Jeevana Karyalaya, Bangalore
2. *Chennabasavanayaka,* 1957, (trans) Navaratna Ramarao, Jeevana Karyalaya, Bangalore
3. *Chikaveera Rajendra,* 1992, (trans) Padma Ramachandra Sharma and Ramachandra Sharma, Penguin India

Some Important Books on Masti

In Kannada

1. *Masti Venkatesha Iyengar*, 1957, L S Seshagiri Rao, Mahatma Gandhi Memorial College, Udupi
2. *Mastiyavara Manodharma*,1970,TiTaSharma,Kavijanashraya, Bangalore

3. *Shri Mastiyavara Kathegalu*, 1971, A N Moorthy Rao, Kavayalaya, Mysore
4. *Shrinivasa*, 1972, Mavinakere Ranganathan, Purogami Sahitya Sangha, Malleshwaram, Bangalore
5. *Shrinivasa Sahitya*, 1974, (ed) Ha Ma Nayak, D V K Murthy, Mysore
6. *Shrinivasara Kadambarigalalli Jeevana Darshana*, 1980, V M Inambar, Bangalore University
7. *Dr Masti Venkatesha Iyengar Avara Chikaveera Rajendra*, 1985, Karnataka Sahitya Akademi
8. *Masti Sanchike*, 1985, a special issue of Prabuddha Karnataka on Masti
9. *Mastiyavara Sahitya*, 1986, (ed) G S Shivarudrappa, Bangalore University
10. *Namma Masti*, 1988, Mavinakere Ranganathan, Purogami Sahitya Sangha, Malleshwaram, Bangalore
11. *Mastiyavara Vimarshe*, 1991, G M Hegde, Srimatha Prakashana, Dharwar
12. *Masti: Jeevana mattu Sahitya*, 1992, L S Seshagiri Rao, Dr Masti Venkatesha Iyengar Centenary Celebrations Committee, Bangalore

In English

1. *Masti Venkatesha Iyengar*, 1974, L S Seshagiri Rao, Institute of Kannada Studies, Mysore

Doctoral Theses

1. *Shrinivasara Kathasahitya*, 1981, Satyanarayana, Mysore University
2. *Mastiyavara Kavya*, 1983, CP Siddhashrama Mysore University

A NOTE ON THE EDITOR

Ramachandra Sharma was born on 28 November, 1925 in Bangalore. He was brought up by his uncle who introduced him to the world of literature when he was very young. He started writing early in his career, and though his first collection of poems, *Hridayageetha* (1952), was only a humble effort, he went on to become a major voice on the Kannada literary scene. He is now regarded as a doyen of modem Kannada literature, and is known for his poems, short stories, plays, and translations. He and Gopalkrishna Adiga were the pioneers of the modernist Navya movement which was a reaction against the Navodaya school of writing.

Ramachandra Sharma has brought a freshness into Kannada poetry and fiction. His second collection of poems, *Elu Suttina Kote* (1953) shook the literary world of Kannada both by its theme and form. Some of Dr Sharma's important collections of poetry are *Hesaragatte, Matu-Mata, Dehalige Banda Hosa Varsha.* He has also published *Gestures*, a volume of poems in English.

Besides poetry, Dr Sharma writes plays, short stories, and essays and has published over twenty-five books. Many of his poems and stories have been translated into several languages.

A translator of repute, Ramachandra Sharma has translated prose and verse from Kannada into English. Among his translations, One *Hundred English Poems of This Century* in Kannada has been well received. With his wife, Padma Sharma, he has translated Masti's novel, *Chikaveera Rajendra* and *Yashawant Chittal's The Boy Who Talked To Trees.* He has received the Karnataka Sahitya Akademi Award and the Katha Award for Translation (1992).

Ramachandra Sharma holds a doctorate in psychology from the University of London and has served with UNESCO as an expert in educational psychology. He now lives in Bangalore.

ABOUT KATHA

Katha, a registered nonprofil organization set up in September 1989, works in the areas of education, publishing and community development and endeavours to spread the joy of reading, knowing and living amongst adults and children. Our main objective is **to enhance the pleasures of reading for children and adults,** for experienced readers as well as for those who are just beginning to read. Our attempt is also to stimulate an interest in lifelong learning that will help the child grow into a confident, self-reliant, responsible and responsive adult, as also to help break down gender, cultural and social stereotypes, encourage and foster excellence, applaud quality literature and translations in and between the various Indian languages and work towards community revitalization and economic resurgence. The two wings of Katha are **Katha Vilasam** and **Kalpavriksham.**

KATHA VILASAM, the Story Research and Resource Centre, was set up to foster and applaud quality Indian literature and take these to a wider audience: through quality translations and related activities like **Katha Books. Academic Publishing**, the **Katha Awards** for fiction, translation and Editing. **Kathakaar** the Centre for Children's Literature. **Katha Barani** – the Translation Resource Centre, the **Katha Translation Exchange Programme, Translation Contests. Kanchi** – the Katha National Institute of Translation promotes translation through **Katha Academic Centres** in various Indian universities. **Faculty Enhancement Programmes** through Workshops, seminars and discussions. **Sishya** – Katha Clubs in colleges. **Storytellers Unlimited** – the art and craft of storytelling and **KathaRasa** – performances, art fusion and other events at the Katha Centre.

KALPAVRIKSHAM, the Centre for Sustainable Learning, was set up to foster quality education that is relevant and fun for children from nonliterate families, and to promote community revitalization and economic resurgence work. These goals crystallized in the development of the following areas of activities. **Katha Khazana** which includes **Katha Student Support Centre, Katha Public School. Katha School of Entrepreneurship, KITES** – the Katha Information Technology and eCommerce School. **Iccha Ghar – The Intel Computer Clubhouse @ Katha. Hamara Gaon** and **The Mandals** – Maa, Bapu, Balika, Balak and Danadini. **Shakti Khazana** was set up for skills upgradation and income generation activities comprising the **Khazana Coop**. Kalpana Vilasam is the cell lor regular research and development of teaching/ learning materials, curricula, syllabi, content comprising **Teacher Training, TaQeEd – The Teachers Alliance for Quality eEducation. Tamasha's World!** comprises **Tamasha! the Children's magazine.** *Dhammakdhum! www.tamasha.org* **and ANU – Animals, Nature and YOU!**

BE A FRIEND OF KATHA

If you feel strongly about Indian literature, you belong with us! KathaNet, an invaluable network of our friends, is the mainstay of all our translationorelated activities. We are happy to invite you to join this ever-widening circle of translation activists. Katha, with limited financial resources, is propped up by the unqualified enthusiasm and the indispensable support of nearly 5000 dedicated women and men.

We are constantly on the lookout for people who can spare the time to find stories for us, and to translate them. Katha has been able to access mainly the literature of the major Indian languages. Our efforts to locate resource people who could make the lesser-known literatures available to us have not yielded satisfactory results. We are specially eager to find Friends who could introduce us to Bhojpuri, Dogri, Kashmiri, Maithili, Manipuri, Nepali, Rajasthani and Sindhi fiction.

Do write to us with details about yourself, your language skills, the ways in which you can help us, and any material that you already have and feel might be publishable under a Katha programme. All this would be a labour oflove, of course' But we do offer a discount of 20% on all our publications to Friends of Katha.

Write to us at -

Katha
A-3 Sarvodaya Enclave
Sri Aurobindo Marg
New Delhi 110017

Call us at: 652 4350. 652 4511
or E-mail us at: info@katha.org

www.ingramcontent.com/pod-product-compliance
Lightning Source LLC
Chambersburg PA
CBHW031325230926
51848CB00001B/99
* 9 7 8 8 1 8 7 6 4 9 5 0 2 *